George Manville Fenn

Sweet Mace

a Sussex legend of the iron times - Vol. 3

George Manville Fenn

Sweet Mace
a Sussex legend of the iron times - Vol. 3

ISBN/EAN: 9783337392130

Printed in Europe, USA, Canada, Australia, Japan

Cover: Foto ©Andreas Hilbeck / pixelio.de

More available books at **www.hansebooks.com**

GRANVILLE CLUB.

SWEET MACE.

SWEET MACE

A SUSSEX LEGEND OF THE IRON TIMES.

BY

G. MANVILLE FENN.

IN THREE VOLUMES.

VOL. III.

LONDON: CHAPMAN & HALL,
LIMITED.
1884.

WESTMINSTER :
NICHOLS AND SONS, PRINTERS,
25, PARLIAMENT STREET.

CONTENTS.

VOLUME III.

CONTENTS.

SWEET MACE.

CHAPTER I.

HOW THE WITCH SAID THERE SHOULD BE NO WEDDING.

"THAT Mother Goodhugh must have a care of herself," said Sir Thomas a day or two later; and Anne let fall her work upon her knee to listen to her father's words.

"And pray why?" said Dame Beckley, who was shaking up some strange infusion of herbs in a bottle.

"I hear strange things of her," said Sir Thomas; "things that, as a justice, I shall be bound to stay."

"And why?" said the dame, as she took

out the stopper and had a long sniff at the contents of the bottle.

"Because they savour of witchcraft and the use of spells. His Majesty has opened a stern commission against such dealings, and as one whom he has delighted to honour I feel bound to show my zeal."

"Fiddle-de-dee!" cried Dame Beckley; "show thy zeal by growing wiser, Thomas. Smell that!"

As the dame held the bottle beneath her lord's nose, Anne glided out of the room, and made her way towards Mother Good-hugh's cot, where she found the old woman ready to meet her with a suspicious look, and, with a feeling of gratified malice, told her of the words her father had let drop.

"But you could stay him, dearie," said the old woman, with a look of terror which she could not conceal.

"Yes. But tell me — what have you done?"

"Wait, dearie, wait," whispered the old woman. "The wedding will never be."

"But it takes place in four days!" cried Anne. "Sir Mark actually dared to come over and tell my father."

"And he told thee, dearie?"

"Nay, he told my mother, and she told me."

"Four days," said the old woman trembling; "four days. The time be short, but it will do. I tell thee the wedding will never be."

"Can I believe thee this time, Mother Goodhugh?" cried the girl excitedly.

"Give me thy word as a lady, that I shall not be ill-treated by thy father and his people, and I swear to you the wedding shall never be."

"There is my hand," said Anne; and, as the old woman held it, there was a strange look on the girl's face as she bent down and

Mother Goodhugh whispered to her for a few minutes, after which she hurried from the cottage.

"And they call me witch, and think me ready to do any evil!" she muttered as she gazed after the girl; "while that young, fairly-formed creature has a heart full of devilry such as never entered mine. But it must be done—it must be done."

She sat brooding over her cold hearth till evening: and then, as soon as it was dark, put on her cloak, took her stick, and walked cautiously to the Pool-house, where she succeeded in getting to the kitchen window unperceived, reaching in and touching Janet on the shoulder with her stick as she sat nodding near it in her chair.

The girl started, and as her eyes fell upon the face of the visitor her lips parted to utter a cry, but the peculiar look on the old woman's face seemed to fascinate her, and she sat back gazing at her as Mother Goodhugh climbed in at the casement, and stood by her side.

"Wh—what do you want?" faltered the girl.

"I've come to see thee, dearie," said the old woman, smiling. "I want to know how you be getting on."

"But you must not stay here!" cried Janet, making an effort to recover herself. "If master knew he would drive me hence."

"Go and tell him, then, child," said Mother Goodhugh mockingly. "Go and tell him that Mother Goodhugh has come to ask thee about thy love affairs, and the philtre she gave thee. What? You will not? He, he, he, he! What a strange girl you are."

"But you must not stay!" cried Janet in alarm. "If you were found here master would never forgive me."

"He is sitting smoking and drinking in

his parlour, dearie, and never comes this way after dark."

" Yes, yes, he does ! " cried the girl ; " he comes sometimes to go down to the powder-cellar with a lantern."

" What, through that door ? " said Mother Goodhugh, pointing.

"Nay, nay! That be the beer cellar. That be the way to the powder-cellar," she said, pointing to a massive door, down a couple of steps. " That be the first door, and there be another farther on at the end of the passage."

" Lawk adear ! " said Mother Goodhugh, " and aren't you afraid, when they bring the stuff down ? "

" They never bring it through here," said the girl. " They let the little barrels down through a hole covered with a flat stone outside there amongst the trees, and master goes along with Tom Croftly to take it, in their slippers, and then comes back and locks it up."

" Ay, and I'll be bound to say always carries the keys in his pocket, eh!"

"No," said the girl, shaking her head. " They hang on a nail in the passage by the door."

" There, I don't want to know about the powder, dearie," cried Mother Goodhugh. " Oh, the horrible stuff! I always begin to curse when I hear it mentioned, so we won't talk about it. I came to see you, and talk about love, and ——"

" But you mustn't stop, indeed you mustn't stop," whispered Janet. " Suppose Mistress Mace should come ? "

" But she won't come, dearie. She's in the corner of the parlour window with the handsome young spark from town."

" How do you know ? " cried Janet.

" How do I know, child! He-he-he! Do you think there's anything I don't know ?

You came to me because I was the wise woman, eh ?"

" Ye-es," faltered the girl.

" Well, didn't you expect me to be wise, child, eh ? "

Janet shrank as far away from her as she could, and stared at her, round of eye and parted of mouth.

" Look here, dearie," whispered the old woman, " don't try to deceive me. I'm such a good friend, but such a bad enemy. You wouldn't like to make me angry, and set me cursing and ill-wishing you."

" N—no," faltered Janet, who began to be horribly frightened of the penetrating eyes that seemed to read her inmost thoughts.

" No, of course you would not. How often did'st say Mas' Cobbe went down into the powder-cellar ? "

" Only once a month," said the girl, " when they've finished working."

" Then he'll be going down directly ? "

"Oh, no; they finished there last week, and it will be three weeks, just," faltered Janet.

"Dear me, will it?" said the old woman. "But, as I was saying, it would be so horrible if I cursed you, though it is not me, my dear, but something in me that does it. It be an evil spirit," she whispered, "and I've known girls as handsome as you lose their round, red cheeks, and soft, smooth skin, and their eyes have grown sunken, and their foreheads wrinkled. It be very horrible, my dear, but I couldn't help it."

Janet tried to get up and go away, but her visitor's fierce, sharp eyes seemed to hold her back in her seat, a fact which Mother Goodhugh well knew and rejoiced in.

It was the only pleasure the old woman had, and she felt at times like this how it recompensed her for the dread she felt of the stringent laws. A curious smile played round her thin lips, and Janet shuddered as the old woman leaned forward till her face was close to that of her victim.

"How is the love going on, dearie?" she whispered.

"Don't—ask—me," faltered the girl.

"You didn't take the stuff, dearie, to give yourself ease?"

"How—how did you know?"

"How did I know? He-he-he!" laughed the old woman, with a cacchination that was enough to freeze the girl's blood. "I know, child, and you can't deceive me. Why didn't you take it?"

"I—I was afraid," stammered Janet. "Mary Goodsell took some once, but it killed her and her baby too."

"Afraid? Stuff! Afraid to give your-self ease when Mistress Mace was torturing you by her love-makings with the fine spark who played with you, and pretended to love you."

"He didn't pretend," said the girl, indignantly. "He did love me till she came between."

"Ah, yes, child, I suppose so; but she be a white witch and very strong, and she would come between and master him. She could lead him wherever she liked, and win him to love her with her spells. Don't trouble your poor, dear heart about him any more, my child, but take the drops, and be happy."

"I—I don't think I dare," faltered the girl.

"Dare? Pish! child, you be too brave and handsome a girl not to dare. It be a pity, too, that she should have come between," said Mother Goodhugh, musingly. "Ah! I have known cases where handsome, noble gentlemen have come down into country places and seen village girls, not so beautiful as thou, child, and married them, and taken them away; and a few years after they have come back looking fine ladies, with their diamonds, and jewels, and carriages, and servants."

Janet's eyes sparkled as this indirect piece of flattery went on.

"I'll take it," she said hastily; "I'll take it."

"Take it? Of course you will, dearie!" cried Mother Goodhugh; "and now look here, my child. I want something of thine to complete a little spell I have at work. Thou hadst a ribbon round thy neck when thou camest to me."

"Yes," said Janet, "a red one; Mas' Wat Kilby gave it to me."

"Nay, then, child, that will not do. I only want an inch cut from it by thy left hand; but if it be tainted by an old man's love it would not do. Let me see. Thou hast not anything given thee by the young court gallant?"

"No," said the girl. Then, with a hasty glance around, she whispered "I have a piece of lace he gave to Mistress Mace, and which she would not wear."

"That will do, child; go, get me the tiniest scrap of that, and I will weave a spell that shall bring thee happiness and peace."

Janet rose and opened the door, and listened.

"They be all in the room," she whispered, as she closed the door again.

"That be well. Be quick. child, and let me get out of this place."

"Thou wilt not move while I am gone."

"Nay, nay, child, not I; but harkye, leave the door ajar while thou art gone up stairs, so that if I hear a step that be not thine I may flee."

Janet looked doubtful for a moment, and then turned to go.

"I need not bring the whole piece?" she whispered.

"Faith, no, child; I'll not rob you of it. The tiniest scrap be all I want. It must be something that the knight has touched."

Janet nodded, and slipped out of the room,

but ere she reached the staircase Mother Goodhugh was at the passage door listening; and, as the last stair creaked beneath the weak girl's tread, the old woman had glided into the passage, peered about by the light of the rush-candle burning on a stand, and uttered a grunt of disappointment. The next moment, though, she saw what she wanted, in the shape of a couple of keys hanging high up, close to the ceiling; and, stepping on a chair, she just reached them, and, lightly crept back along the passage to sit down in the kitchen, panting from exertion and excitement combined.

Before she could compose herself Janet was back, too much excited herself to notice the old woman's hurried breathings.

" I've got it," she cried, producing a handsome piece of lace. " I must cut some off here. Be quick; I be in such a fright for fear some one should come."

" That will do, dearie," said the old

woman, tearing off a scrap from one end. "There, put it away, and let me begone. Take the drops, child, and give thyself ease. You don't care for such love as his."

Janet did not reply, but gladly opened the door to get rid of her unwelcome visitor, who stepped out into the dark night, and hurried away across the little bridge, and into the lane, where she turned to shake her stick at the peaceful-looking house, with its lighted windows.

" Now we shall see—now we shall see ! " she cried. " Two ways open, and my sayings coming to pass. There will be no wedding now."

CHAPTER II.

HOW CULVERIN CARR SEALED UP THE STORE.

THE autumn sun shone brightly down into the ravine that led up to the mouth of Gil Carr's store, and the steep sides were glorious with the bright berries that glistened amongst the changing leaves. Where the briony, with its bronze green foliage, flung down its wreaths, there was cluster after cluster of orange scarlet fruit. The brambles hung down thorny strands black with rich ripeness that there was no hand to gather; and wherever a prickly holly, all glistening glossy green, had rooted in some crevice of the sand-rock, it was covered with yellow berries awaiting more kisses from the ardent sun before blushing scarlet for the Christmastide.

The ferns were beginning to be dappled on their dark green fronds with gorgeous dashes of orange and chrome, mingled with crimson, red as blood, and the dyes of the finger-leaved maple were nearly as bright. Where the white tails of the rabbits could be seen disappearing as their owners heard a tramp of many feet, the dense small-leaved sloe-bushes, with their cruel thorns, showed many a row of tiny plums of the richest violet, dusted with a delicate pearly bloom. The late blossoms of the yellow ragwort clustered amidst the purple heath, and glossy ivy hung in strands swinging in the hot sunshine with the tender tips just brushing the seeded grass self-turned into useless hay.

Hot, still, and breathless lay the ravine, with all its natural riches, ripe with the fullness of the season, and now resting, waiting the coming of the cold wintry winds, that, sweeping up from the sea, should beat and tear and bear away the brightness of the autumn and turn all to desolation and death.

Suddenly a velvety blackbird, with its orange bill and yellow-circled eyes, uttered its alarm-note and flew along like a streak of night away up and along the side of the ravine to the over-hanging woods. A chat that had been busy twittering its song over a golden clump of furze stopped half-way and dived amongst the purple heath, while a glistening lizard, that had half taken the alarm from the scattering rabbits, ran beneath the leaves.

The steps in the distance grew plainer on the ear, and a greeny olive snake raised its head where it lay in a twirl upon a shelf of short, fine, sun-browned turf, darted its tongue out over its hard shiny jaws, and glided under the root of a tree, seeming to give warning of danger by its low hiss to an adder higher up the stony way, for the little viper condescended to raise its head where it lay like a scaly letter S upon the mossy stump of a hazel bush, round whose green, mouldering, gnarled stem were clustered, like chalices, so many thickly-veined fungi that looked as if roughly cast in orange-tinted deadened gold.

The danger seemed to be far off, for the viper lay down its spade-shaped head once more, yawned, and seemed disposing itself for another sunny sleep, but had hardly arranged its tail to its satisfaction when—*rustle—tap*—something fell from above, and struck it sharply on the back.

It was only a hazel nut that could hang no longer in its husk, but ripened into a soft warm brown, it had dried and dried till a leaf or two above it had ceased to give its shade, and then it had fallen like a warning upon the viper's back.

A moment before and the little reptile was sluggishness itself; this blow, light as it was, seemed to galvanise it into life, for a quick spasm darted through it, there was a sharp wave, and the raised head was ready to strike, while the eyes, that had a moment before resembled dim oxidised silver, now glittered like tiny jewels, as the whole creature seemed to become the picture of malicious rage, and sought where to drive deep its poison-fangs.

There was somehow a kind of resemblance between the little serpent and Anne Beckley, though there was no one by to see, as, failing an object at which to strike, the reptile seemed to consider that discretion was the better part of valour; and, slowly lowering its crest, it threw its body into a series of horizontal waves, and gradually disappeared beneath some tawny - golden bracken on the slope.

The steps came nearer, and suddenly there

was a movement on the edge of the cliff, high above the store, where a bronzed man took his place, evidently on the look-out.

Directly after another was seen scaling the side of the ravine to post himself on the slope over the entrance, while again another suddenly appeared amidst the furze on the green shoulder which overlooked the sloping downs.

Gil Carr's men did not often visit the place by day, hence the precautions against being watched by some intruder.

High up above the cavern, the gaunt figure of Wat Kilby suddenly showed against the sky. Then he shrank down into a little depression half overgrown with trees, and soon after a thin, pale blueish vapour arose, and kept rising, as, pipe in mouth, the old sailor seated himself upon a block of stone to watch.

Meanwhile, up the bottom of the ravine, close down by where the clear stream wandered in its deep fern-hung mossy shades, a little party of some twenty men wound their way.

Every man seemed well armed, and, with the exception of their leader, all appeared to be carrying a burden, either a small keg or a little chest, or a heavy packet, which they bore through the clustering bushes, which seemed to interlace their arms and try to stay them as they forced their way amongst the rocks.

After climbing pretty close to the end, at a word from Gil the loads were set down, arms laid aside, and by means of half a dozen pike-staves the great stone was rolled away.

The men then waited while Gil went in and lit a lanthorn, returning soon after to make a sign, when one by one they all lifted and bore in their loads, following their leader for some distance to where the dim light showed an inner cavern, whose sides and roof had evidently been roughly chiselled out by the hands of man.

Here the fresh additions to the stores of the place were neatly deposited, and the sailors sat down, while Gil busied himself in examining a bale or two that seemed to have been gnawed by rats.

" I wonder where the skipper shoved that spying fellow Churr —him as we searched for ?" said one of the men in a low voice to his nearest comrade.

" Further in, somewhere," was the reply ; " I thought I could smell him just now."

"That be rats," said the other ; "I know them well enough. But does the place go in far ? "

" I believe you, my lad. I once went in ever so far with old Wat and the skipper carrying lanterns."

" Did you ?" said the other, eagerly ; " and what be it like ? "

" Like this here. All the same—hole

after hole, with rough stone pillars to support it all, just as it must have been dug out."

" Bah! chap, this was never cut out," said the other.   " It came natural like."

" Never cut out?   Come natural like? Look here, my lad," said the sailor, rising and pointing to marks upon the wall that seemed to have been made with some rough tool.

" Yes, but anybody might have done that," said the younger man.

" You can think what you like," said the other.   " I'm telling you what the skipper told old Wat, and you never knew him tell a lie. He said to old Wat, ' My father found the way rabbiting when a boy, and forgot all about it till he felt the want of a place to store things in unknown to other folk, and then he recollected this.' He said it was made by folks as lived underground hundreds of thousands of years ago."

" Oh ? " said the other.

" Yes; and they dug first one and then another, as they wanted them, and grew bigger in numbers, and that it went right in farther than they'd ever been on account of the bad air."

" Same as down among the bilge in the ship's hold ?"

" That's so.   The skipper's father was most stifled by it once when he tried to go right in."

" But do they go right in ?"

The elder sailor struck the top of an empty barrel a sharp rap with the hilt of his sword, and the other's question was answered, for the sound went echoing into the distance till it died away.

" It be a queer sort of place," said the other, with a half shudder. " Hang me if I'd like to be boxed up here along with Abel Churr, if the skipper's stowed him there."

" Plenty of room and good water," said

the other, pointing down to where the source
of the stream outside ran trickling through
the interstices of the stone, and formed tiny
pools of limpid clearness.

"Ugh! the place smells damp and cold,
and I should expect to come out, if I was
shut up here, all over blue mould."

"Like a bit of ship's cheese, eh? Come
along: here's the skipper."

"Now, my lads!" cried Gill, just then,
" work with a will, plenty to do."

He led the way, and the men followed
him with a sense of relief out into the bright
sunshine, where the ferns fringed the rough
arch over the entrance to the hole.

They glanced at the heaps of stores and
the various shipping chandlery, spare sails
and cordage, but all was so familiar that
nothing excited their interest.

Just as they reached the outside there was
a whistle from below, and Gil uttered an
impatient ejaculation. But hurrying a little

distance down, he peered over a mass of rock, to see one of his men, who had been on sentry, leading a dark figure with bandaged eyes.

" Father Brisdone ! " said Gil. " Bring him along, my lad."

Going forward, he quickly undid the handkerchief and threw it aside.

" I forgot to tell them, father," he said, holding out his hand; " there was no need with you."

" I do not wish to pry into any of your secrets, my son, that you do not care to trust me with," said Father Brisdone, smiling as he took the young man's hand.

" Trust you, father ? Why, I'd trust you with anything. But you look weary and hot with your journey. Sit down on yon stone : this is nature's parlour. Here is something to eat. Lockyer, a bottle of that wine from the case inside on the left. The cup too."

Leading the father to a nook by the side of the entry, he placed refreshments before him, and then said—

"Now you shall see us lock up the house, for it may be a year before we return."

"Why should you show me?" said Father Brisdone, smiling.

"Why should I not show the man whom I have always looked upon as a trusty friend?" retorted Gil. "Now, my lads," he said, and, leaving the father's side, he soon had his men busy with spade and shovel. First of all the old stone was reared into its place. Then smaller blocks were thrust in here and there, so as to completely wedge it in. Then shovels of stones were thrown into fissures, and sods of earth, mingled with grass and heather, were carefully arranged; after which broad-fronded ferns, roots of rag-wort, grasses, and bramble roots were planted, dead leaves sprinkled here and there, and touch after touch given till nothing seemed left to be done but to pour water over the new earth to bind it together, and make the plants take root.

" There," said Gil to the father, as he stopped by him, hot and panting; " unless some spy has watched our work, that is safe enough, for in a week's time those things will be growing again."

" Yes, that will be secure enough," said the father, rising. " Thanks, my son, I was indeed faint for want of food. And now, what next ? "

" Next, father, you will accompany my man there on board. The little ship lies ready in the river ; he will take you down in the skiff. If all's well we shall be with you soon after midnight, and then heaven send us favouring gales, for we shall drop down the river on the tide, and put to sea at once."

" But no bloodshed, my son. For heaven's sake do not let the hand that leads your promised wife on board be red with the blood of a fellow-man."

" Father," said Gil, sternly, " I am no cut-throat; I am no lover of the sword. I go to-night to fetch my wife, and I go with peace and love towards all; but if that man or his followers stand in my path to prevent us, they must take what follows, for I cannot trifle now."

Father Brisdone sighed.

" You know the consequences; if I do not get her away to-night, they are to be wed at eight o' the clock, and to stay that, there must be a deadly fray. Trust me, father; and, if I can help it, no blood shall be shed."

" I trust you, my son. Go, and my blessing be with you. I shall make the little cabin a chapel, where I shall pass the time in prayer for your success."

" And then, father, a chapel where you make her mine by ties that none can break."

" Amen, my son, amen!" said Father Brisdone ; and they parted, the father to follow his guide down the valley, and Gil to lead his men through one of the forest tracks in the direction of Roehurst Pool, Wat and the other watchers closing in behind.

The advance was made with caution to within a mile of the foundry, where, beneath a spreading oak, Gil called a halt, and cast his eyes over his party of twenty sturdy, well-armed men, every one of whom could handle his weapon well.

" That will do, my lads," he said in his quick, imperious way. " Now lie down, and eat and rest. Silence, every man ; not a word above a whisper. Goodsell, Kingley, two hundred paces each of you along the track. A good look - out, and a quick whistle, if so much as a berry-hunting child approach."

His orders were carried out, and then with the soft autumn evening rapidly drawing nigh, Gil also went out through the forest to watch and listen for the approach of footsteps that might end in the discovery of his men.

CHAPTER III.

HOW GIL AND HIS MEN DREW SWORD.

THE hours glided slowly by, and the soft damp of night scented the forest with its peculiar odours,—of decaying leaves, swift-growing fungi, and mouldering wood. Ever and again a leaf that had hung lightly by its dying stalk became so laden with dew that it fell pattering down with a noise that seemed startlingly loud in the silence of the time.

Borne on the sighing breeze that whispered through the branches above came, rising and falling, the rushing sound of falling water, as the swift stream dashed past the front of the founder's house, and hurried towards the huge wheel, but only to be turned aside to sweep with a sudden plunge into the lower hole.

There was something very strange and hollow that night in the sound of the rushing stream ; and, as Gil stood leaning against a tree, the falling water seemed now distant, dying away in sighs ; now close at hand, rolling down with a thunderous bass. If he had been asked why it affected him, he could not have said ; but its deep notes sounded then like a portent of mishap. He remembered it afterwards so well, for every incident of that memorable evening seemed to be burned into his brain, and he had but to lean over the side of his ship and gaze away into the depths of air and sea to have all come vividly back as if the events were then taking place.

Hour after hour glided by and there was no interruption, nothing to disturb the soli-tude. From time to time Gil walked back to the oak, but only to find his men well on the alert, and that the sentries had nothing to report. There was scarcely any talking, no drinking, and no smoking, for his people were in earnest to do everything possible to carry out their leader's plans. Even Wat Kilby contented himself with sucking quietly at his empty pipe and glancing round at every man in turn to see that the rules were kept.

Hardly a word had passed between Wat and his leader, for the old man was in dudgeon. He had had his shrewd suspicions that Gil intended to carry off Mace that night, and he had come to the conclusion that his duty was to take Janet at the same time. To his anger and disgust, though, he found that this was strictly forbidden, and earlier in the day a sharp verbal contest had ensued.

" Why can't I take her abroad ? " he growled. " You're going to have a priest, and I want a wife same as other men."

"Once for all, Wat," said Gil, sternly; "I will have no paltering with the work I have on hand. Will you obey me and work to the end for my scheme?"

"Why, of course I will," grumbled the old fellow; "but I don't see why as——"

"Not another word!" cried Gil.

"But what I says is this, skipper: Thou'st got a priest——"

"Silence, sir; how dare you!" roared Gil; and the old man shrank away to pull out his little pipe, and begin sucking at it viciously, jerking his long body about, and acting generally as if he had a volcanic eruption going on within him, the safety-valve to which was an explosion of muttered words now and then, which escaped after a kind of quake that shook him like a spasm from top to toe.

All the same, though, Wat made no further resistance to his leader's will, but with the energy of a long tried, well-disciplined follower, he worked away at the various preparations, and was as obedient as a dog.

As Gil stood thinking in the wood, he once more went over his plans, wondering whether there would be an encounter with Sir Mark's followers, and then smiling grimly to himself, as he half wished there might be, and thought of how he would like once more to stand face to face with the man who was so nearly robbing him of her whom he had always looked upon as his very own.

At last the time seemed to him to be a fitting one for the venture, and, giving the signal, his men started up from amongst the dewy herbage; there was the clink of arms and a rustling noise as all fell into their places; and, taking the head of his little force, Gil gave his final orders, especially commanding silence, and made for the Pool-house.

Gil's plans were well matured, and his followers fell into their respective places without confusion. Arriving pretty close to the foundry, he posted them behind the smallest of the furnace-sheds, where the black shadow of night was blacker than in the open ; and then, with Wat at his elbow, he made for another shed, where he knew that a short stout ladder was kept.

This was in its place, and Wat was about to shoulder it, when in a low hoarse whisper the old fellow said :—

" You'll let me take her, too, skipper ? "

For answer Gil turned angrily.

" Put that ladder down," he whispered ; " and go back. Send Morris."

" No, no, skipper," whispered the old fellow hastily. " Let me go."

" Put down the ladder. Go back, and send me a trustworthy man."

" I'm the trustworthiest man you've got, skipper," growled Wat, " only I was obliged to say a word for I feel as I ought to marry the girl now. You don't know what it is to be in love, skipper, or you would not treat me thus."

" Do you go, or stay ?" said Gil.

"Stay," said Wat. "I shan't leave you, skipper, come what may. I've done. Not another word about it will you hear from me."

Wat shouldered the ladder, and together the two men walked towards the water-run, and along it by the stones to the little bridge, which they softly crossed, and entered the garden.

They paused to listen, but all was very still and dark. A more suitable night could not have been chosen for the adventure, and together they made for Mace's window, where a dim light was burning.

The end of the ladder rustled slightly as it was borne amongst the trees, and they again stopped to listen; but all was still, and so intense was the darkness now before moonrise—the moon that was to light the boat down the river to where the ship lay waiting --that they could see neither to the right nor the left, even the thick bushes under the window were in the gloom.

Would she fail him at this important time ? Gil's heart asked; but he crushed down the thought. No : she would come, he was sure of it, for she had promised him, and he felt no fear of her wanting in spirit for the enterprise.

"No," he muttered; "she would go through fire and water to escape his touch alone, and she would dare more to be beside me."

There was a thrill of joy at these thoughts, and he gazed anxiously at the window, waiting to see it opened, that he might raise the ladder and help her away.

It must be the hour, he thought, but the next minute he set it down to impatience.

" She will be to her time," he said.

As if warned by an instinct of coming danger, Gil Carr drew his sword, and, resting the point upon the toe of his boot, stood leaning his hands upon the hilt, while Wat placed the foot of the ladder on a flower-bed, and held the two sides, with his rusty beard upon one of the spokes, thinking of how he wished they were going to carry off Janet, and whether she would have been willing to come.

"She did call me an old fool last time, and slapped my face," he muttered; "but that was only by way of showing how fond she was. Ha! it be terrifying work having to deal with such an arbitrary skipper as ourn."

Gil still gazed at the window, thinking that if he had changed places with Sir Mark, and a dangerous foe had been in the field, a cordon of sentries would have been placed round the house for his love's protection; whilst Sir Mark was evidently sleeping luxuriously, and dreaming, perhaps, of possessing his fair young bride. "Poor, befooled idiot!" said

Gil to himself; " I do not envy him his morrow's waking. Why, if I——. Pst! Wat, your sword."

His left hand involuntarily flew to the silver whistle that hung at his neck, while his sword was raised readily, and turned aside a pass that grazed his ribs. For in an instant the bushes around them seemed alive with armed men, who rose in obedience to a call, and made for Gil and his old follower.

Wat was as much upon the alert as his leader, but he had not time to draw his sword. Not that it mattered, for the short ladder became a very effective weapon in the emergency. Raising it with both hands above his head, he poised it there for a moment, keeping it well ready, and then, darting it rapidly forward again and again, he drove it into the chests of three or four assailants, sending them crashing down amongst the bushes, as he kept them sufficiently distant to prevent them from reaching him with the points of their swords.

As the first blade gritted against that of Gil's, he placed the whistle to his lips, and its note rang out shrilly on the midnight air, to be answered by the rush of feet over the little wooden bridge as his men came running up; and now there was nothing left but for the defenders of the house to be beaten back, the place itself to be forced, and Mace carried away.

"Swing the bridge!" cried a voice, which Gil recognised as that of Sir Mark. "They're trapped now. Hollo, there! Lights, quick! Surrender, you dogs, in the King's name."

There was a creaking noise as the little bridge was swung round, and Gil felt that, far from being in sleepy indolence and safety, Sir Mark had not only been well on the alert, but had cleverly made his plans according to his own lights to entrap his rival and his followers when they came, attracted, as he felt that they would be, by the bait within the founder's house.

"Poor fool!" muttered Gil, "if he thinks he can take us here."

For his men came running to his side to group round where he and Wat were standing well at bay.

CHAPTER IV.

HOW THE POWDER HAD ITS SAY.

Sir Mark had not been alone in his suspicions, for the founder had had a half fancy come into his head that Gil might make some effort to prevent the marriage; and after all he could not help feeling that he would not be sorry if this were done. Now it had come so near he thought more than ever that he was doing wrong in giving his consent, for Mace's distress seemed to be ever on the increase, and he dreaded losing his child.

"But it's too late now," he muttered—" too late. Matters must go on as they are, and it will be a grand and good thing for my little girl to become my lady—Dame Leslie, who will take her place at Court with the finest of them there."

" Do you think our friend Culverin will show himself at the wedding to-morrow ?" Sir Mark said.

" I cannot help thinking that he will," said the founder.

" Well, for my part," said Sir Mark, " I have a suspicion that we shall see him sooner —that he will make an effort to carry her off to-night."

" Nay !" cried the founder, flushing, " he would not dare."

" I think he would," said Sir Mark, with a cunning smile. " Why look, man, what easier ? He has followers and a vessel. Depend upon it, he will try to get our darling away to his ship."

" If he dared to attempt such an outrage," cried the founder, half rising from his seat;

and then, as if changing his mind, he sat
back thoughtfully in his chair.

" You would spit him, eh, Master Cobbe ?
A most worthy proceeding. But, look here,
I have made my plans."

" Plans ? "

" Yes. I have, as you know, six men
here, all well armed, and to do honour to
my wedding a gentleman of His Majesty's
household, a friend of mine, will be here
this evening, as soon as it is dusk, with
eighteen fighting-men beside. These will
come unseen, when I give the signal, and be
placed in ambush in the garden. I shall
plant two by the open bridge, and, if our
friend comes, he and his men will walk into
a trap, for the moment they are over, the
bridge will be closed, and thus, you see, my
dear father-in-law elect, I shall rid myself of
an awkward rival, and his Majesty of a band
of buccaneers.

"But there will be bloodshed, and on the eve of my child's wedding."

"Pish!" cried Sir Mark. "Have no fear of that. Once the rats are in the trap, and they will shriek for mercy, as such ruffians and bullies always do. My dear father-in-law, you shall have the pleasure of seeing the whole band tied two and two, and marched off, when the district will be cleared."

"And my business ruined," said the founder.

"Trust me for that, old man," said Sir Mark, smiling. "You shall make culverins and howitzers for his Majesty's troops to your heart's content, so have no fear. Powder shall you manufacture, too, but we will not talk of that. Did his Majesty know that powder was stored upon your place, ay, ever so little, he would never be your friend. But how do you like my plans?"

"Not well," said the founder, gloomily. "I liked Gil. You rob him of the woman he meant to be his wife. Why take his liberty as well?"

"Master Cobbe, this is wretched drivel," cried Sir Mark, laying his hand upon his shoulder. "What am I to think of it?"

"What you will," said the founder, sullenly; "I like not my part at all."

"And you will betray my plans?" said Sir Mark, angrily.

"Nay!" exclaimed the founder, sharply, as something of his old mien showed itself in his countenance. "Sir Mark Leslie, I am a rough yeoman of the country, but I have something of the gentleman at my heart. You insult me by your suspicions. I gave you my word, and my hand upon it, that my child should be your wife, and I repent me of it now; but Jeremiah Cobbe is not the man to go back from his word, and, sooner than Gil Carr should forcibly carry her away, I'd take him myself, and deliver him into your hand."

"I did but jest, father," said Sir Mark, grasping the founder's hand. "Now, let us see something of pretty little Mace for an hour, before I perfect my plans."

Janet was summoned, but she announced that her mistress was busy preparing things for her departure, and the girl hurried back to Mace's room, to gloat over the silk dresses and presents that lay about.

Other messages were sent to Mace in the course of the evening, but she refused to come, and at last, out of patience, as the soft autumn night began to fall, Sir Mark went out to finish his arrangements.

"You are master, to-day, my lady," he muttered; "to-morrow I shall rule, and you'll know it too."

Had Gil dared to post a man nearer to the house, he would have known of the preparations made to entrap him, though possibly they would not have kept him back. As it was he knew nothing of the well-armed soldiers who, punctual to the moment, marched across the bridge, and were rapidly disposed in suitable places by Sir Mark, who exhibited no mean generalship in his plans.

Then came the waiting, and Sir Mark stood listening with the founder by his side.

"They'll not come," said the latter, impatiently, after a weary while.

"Hist! there is one," whispered Sir Mark, as a footstep cautiously crossed the bridge.

"Why it is a woman," said the founder.

"A disguise," replied Sir Mark. "Gil himself."

"Nay, it is Mother Goodhugh. I know her walk and her tap with her stick. The old hag! I'll go and turn her back. What does she want?"

"Bah! be silent, man; she comes to see the maids—fortune-telling, or to beg for something in the way of cakes or wine. I'll not have my plans spoiled now. Hist! what's that?"

It was a heavier foot this time, and unmis-takeably Gil and a companion had arrived. Then followed the rustling of the ladder, the waiting, the signal whistle, and, when the bridge had been closed, Sir Mark's summons to surrender.

Lights flashed upon the dark scene as Sir Mark's command rang out, and Gil saw that he and his men were far outnumbered.

He stamped his foot impatiently, for, though he felt no fear of being beaten, the presence of these men might hinder the carrying out of his plans.

"Surrender, you dog!" roared Sir Mark again. "In the King's name, I say. Shoot down every man who resists."

A scornful roar of laughter was the response; and, as the heavy guns of the period were levelled, Gil's men, lithe and active as wild cats, leaped at their bearers with their swords, dashing the guns up, so that the scattered volley that followed sent the bullets skyward, while man after man was knocked down by a blow or the recoil of the piece.

Then commenced a furious fight; sword clashed with sword; there were groans, oaths, and cries; and, as Mace's casement was opened, its occupant gazed down, shuddering at the hideous, torch-lit scene in the trampled garden.

"Be ready with that ladder, Wat," cried Gil, hoarsely. "She must be got away now at any cost. Hah! there is Sir Mark."

As he uttered the words he sprang at his rival, who had recognised him at the same moment by the flickering light of one of the torches borne by a soldier, who held it on high as he tried to take aim at Wat Kilby with a wheel-lock pistol, from beneath Mace's window.

"Surrender!" shouted Sir Mark. "Quick, here, men, here!"

"Surrender yourself," roared Gil, as with

a rush he beat aside the other's guard, closed with him, and forced him down, where he lay with Gil's knee at his throat.

Their leader's cry, though, brought half a-dozen men to his side, and blade in hand they would have cut down Gil had it not been for Wat, whose orders had been to stay there with the ladder. Raising this, he drove it with a crash against one man, who had raised his point, and was in the act of striking another, when Sir Mark recovered himself sufficiently to get at a dagger, which he would have plunged into his opponent, had he not felt himself scorched by a blinding glare, as he, Gil, and Wat and those by him were hurled headlong amongst the trampled bushes, and, before they could realise what had happened, there was a mighty roar, as if thunder had come from earth instead of sky, and then gone rolling across the Pool, to die away in echoes amongst the hills.

CHAPTER V.

HOW THE LOVE PHILTRE WORKED.

If Mother Goodhugh had stood by while it was done, Janet the weak would have taken the decoction placed in her hands; but, foolish as the girl was, she had her share of cunning.

"If I give it to her and it does make her love turn to hatred, he must turn to me; and, if after all she cares more for Captain Carr, why even then it may turn right for me. Does the old thing think I'd take the stuff? Clever as she be, others be clever too. But how shall I give it to her?"

Janet took the little flask out of her bosom,

which was her hiding-place for particular things—·ribbons, scraps of lace, a scent-bottle wonderfully like one of Mace's—and looked at it attentively.

"A little every day," she said; and the next morning she poured a portion into a jug that stood for drinking purposes in her mistress's room.

That afternoon Mace went up to her bed-room with a bunch of flowers from the garden, which she placed in a shallow basin, and the contents of the jug were used to keep them alive!

The same evening, finding the jug empty, Janet refilled it, and again poured in a little of the contents of the flask.

She had just completed her task when she heard Mace's step upon the stairs, and in her haste to replace the stopper of the flask she let it fall upon the floor, where it broke; and she had only time to throw the broken glass out of the window, and drag a piece of carpet over the stain on the floor, before her mistress entered the room.

Janet escaped as soon as possible and sought refuge in the kitchen, from whence she stole round to the garden and picked up the broken bottle, then ran back, throwing the pieces into the water-race as she hurried along.

"I dare say she will have taken enough," she said to herself, "and, if she has not, I'll try no more. I hate myself for doing it. Poor girl, she looks more as if she was going to be buried than married."

In fact, Janet's heart was not very deeply touched, and she would have been ready to hand over her young affections to anybody a little more eligible than Master Wat Kilby, who was rather too old for her taste. During these busy days, too, there was so much to take her attention, for she had all a girl's love and excitement in an approaching wedding.

First and foremost there came a present to her from Sir Mark in the shape of what was to her a most handsome dress.

" That's for thee, pretty Janet," he said; "and when we come back from our wedding jaunt I'll bring thee a handsome husband as sure as I live. One kiss for it," he said; and he took it, and another and another. How many dozens he would have taken it is impossible to say, only the founder's step was heard, and Janet fled with her dress by another way.

"The spell be working somehow," she said to herself joyously. " May be he will turn her over yet, and marry me himself."

She hurried up to her room to inspect her gown-piece, and smooth her ruffled hair.

" Oh, these men, how wicked they be!" she cried half-petulantly, as she gazed at her flushed cheeks in a damp-stained mirror.

" I be handsomer than mistress pale-face down stairs," she cried, giving her head a toss. "Fie on her! why does she not go and wed with Captain Culverin, and leave me Sir Mark."

The gown-piece again took her attention, and she folded it in pleats and tucks, and draped herself in it, ending by doubling it over and over, and laying it flat beneath her bed.

"I'll go see her presents now," she said; and she descended to Mace's room to find the jug untouched.

"Perhaps she'll never wear these gauds after all," muttered Janet, as she went to the dressing-table and examined the presents Sir Mark had brought, rich jewels some of them, with laces and ribbons enough for a dozen weddings; but the white satin dress hanging across a chair was the great attraction for Janet, with its puckers and folds, and great stomacher dotted with pearls.

"It be brave!" she cried, as she went down upon her knees to gaze at it, and lay portions of the skirt across her arm, or feel its softness against her cheek.

And so the time glided on till the eve of the wedding, when, pale and dark of eye with want of sleep, Mace felt that the excitement was more than she could bear.

It was very terrible, she told herself, and again and again she asked her conscience whether she was doing wisely in listening to Gil's prayers. It was an act of disobedience to her father, whom she dearly loved, and yet she felt that she clung to her lover more. But even now she would, in obedience to her father's wishes, have refused Gil and remained unwed. To be forced, though, to become the wife of one whom she utterly detested she felt was impossible, and she knew that she must go.

She had no one to counsel, none to take her part; and she knelt down and sobbed bitterly as she thought of the mother who had been taken away so long ago.

Then rising from her knees, quite calm and peaceful at heart, she sat down in her sweet-scented old chamber waiting, for she told herself it was inevitable, and that time would soften her father's anger, and all be happiness once more.

"He feels it is for my welfare," she said, "but he does not know poor Gil."

The whispered mention of Gil's name sent a thrill through her, and, with a smile of hope and love upon her worn, pale face, she sat dreaming of him, and mentally praying that no mishap might accompany their flight.

At last, feeling flushed and hot, she drank from the jug of water which Janet had left unchanged.

There was a peculiar taste in it, but her thoughts were too much occupied to pay much attention, and, taking her seat by the window, she sat, watching the darkness coming on of this the last day in her old home.

How the old happy hours of the past came back to torture her with their recollections; and now she told herself it would have been better that she should have died young, in peace and innocency, ere she knew the bitter heart-grievings of the present. For in these last hours her breast was racked by contending emotions; the love of parent fought hard with the stronger, more engrossing love of the maiden for the man of her choice, but the latter won.

Agitated as she was, it seemed to her that she grew feverish and thirsty—a thirst she turned to the water-vessel more than once to assuage, but without effect; and at last, with a curious, excited sensation upon her, mingled with weariness, she went to the glass to find that her cheeks were flushed, and that there was a strange dilated look about her eyes, whose unusual lustre startled her.

"I have had too little sleep lately," she said, with a sad smile, as she thought of the long, restless nights she had passed; and at last she threw herself upon the bed, and closed her eyes, just as a tap was heard upon the panel of the door.

"Come in, Janet," she said, as she unclosed her eyes to gaze round at the confusion that reigned with half-packed garments, and upon a couch her wedding-dress, facing her like the flaccid shade of herself lying upon a bier.

There was something very weird in that dress, and it seemed to influence her with thoughts of death which made her shudder.

"I be come to try on the wedding robe again, mistress," said Janet. "I did alter those strings and that fastening, and now it will fit you well."

"That's kind of you, Janet," said Mace,

drowsily. Thank you for all you have done. You will think kindly of me when I am gone?"

"Why, of course, mistress. But, there, dear heart alive, don't talk like that. Why it be as if you was going to be buried. La! You ought to be as blithe as blithe."

"Should you be, Janet?" said Mace. "Oh, my head—my head, it burns—it burns!"

"La, mistress, yes; as joyous as a bird to wed with so handsome and courtly a man. Art ill, mistress?"

"Sleepy, Janet, sleepy."

"There, then, let's get on the dress, and see how you look, and then you shall have a long sleep, and I'll see that no one disturbs you."

"No, no," said Mace, hoarsely. "I must not sleep, child—I will not sleep. Try on the dress and go away. I shall sit by the open window."

"La, mistress, thou'lt get the ager-shakes

that come off the Pool. I wouldn't sit by the open window to-night. Come, get up, dear, and let me take off your gown. I'll unlace it, and now we'll have on the beautiful white robe. Lovely, lovely!"

And again, "Lovely, lovely!"

And then, "How beautiful you look!"

And amidst it all strange reelings of the brain, her head throbbing and wild imaginings rushing through her mind. She was married and clasped in her lover's arms, and his kisses were showered on her lips, her veins tingled, a strange thrill ran through her nerves, but his kisses burned her face, her eyes, her head. And now it was not Gil who clasped her in the ecstasy of love, but Sir Mark, and, in place of burning passion, she froze, her heart seemed to stand still, and she was numbed with horror as he approached his lips to hers. Why did he laugh so with such a strange, silent, ghastly laugh? Why did he press her so tightly to his breast? His arms hurt her, his breast was bony, and his laugh was lifeless. It was a frightful grin, and she could not tear herself away. It was not Sir Mark; it was a hideous skeleton, and she made a supreme effort to rid herself of the terrible vision that clasped her to its breast.

At last it was gone, and she was dressed in her bridal robe. She was feverish and excited, and that was a kind of nightmare dream. There she was, then, before the big swing mirror, gay in satin and lace, and once more the exclamations of pleasure fell upon her ears.

" How lovely ! how lovely !"

And again, " How beautiful you look !"

The reflection in the mirror died away, for her eyes closed. She could not bear to look upon it longer, and, now that her eyes were shut, once more came the phantoms of her troubled, reeling brain. Gil, Sir Mark, the hideous shape of death, all had her clasped in their arms in turn. She struggled in spirit, but her body was motionless; the brain was in full action, but muscle and nerve were inert. She could only lie there and suffer tortures so horrible that she felt that if they lasted she must go mad.

Then again she was gazing at herself in the great mirror, gay with satin and lace, and once more there was the round of horrors.

How long was it to last?

There was a lucid moment when she knew that she was seriously ill. Some terrible ailment had seized her, and then came the recollection of the water like a flash through her reeling brain.

Was it poison?

" How beautiful! It is lovely, lovely, lovely!" and there was the vision again of the satin gown.

" I must be going mad," she thought; " but Janet must not see. I will be firm and wait. I must send her away soon. Let me see," she thought. "Gil will be here at midnight. I am not too ill to go with him, and, when once away in peace, I shall soon be well. How absurd to think of poison. How beautiful I look. This fever seems to have given me my colour once again. Poor fool! Why should I masquerade like this, when I am never to wear these things? It is time I put them off and sent her away. My poor head, my poor head! how it burns and throbs and reels with pain."

Then again, the wedding with Gil, and his hot kisses burning her face. No, it was Sir Mark; and then again the chilly horror of being seized by those arms and pressed nearer, nearer, to that hideous framework of ghastly bones, while the cold grinning teeth rested against her lips, and in place of kisses began to tear and rend her. Now it was her fair young cheek, now her soft bosom; and at every contact it was the burning pain of ice that froze with a touch like heated iron. She strove to struggle, to call for help, but it was in vain. The hideous teeth were now meeting in her forehead, and a pang of agony ran through her brain.

"Gil, Gil, help me, help!" she tried to say; and then there was the clash of arms, the firing of guns, the shouts of contending men—cries, oaths, shrieks, wails. What was it? Was she really mad? Had her sufferings robbed her of reason, or was she striving to rush from the room down the broad old staircase when that hideous rush of fire, and that crash of thunder, came to tear her away? Was it madness, a dream, or was it——. Her reeling senses seemed to leave her as she asked herself the final question, when she was stricken down, even as her lips uttered the question.

Was it death?

CHAPTER VI.

HOW GIL BROUGHT THE BRIDE FROM THE BURNING HOUSE.

FOR a few moments Gil's men and the followers of Sir Mark stood appalled by the effects of the explosion. Fully one-half had been prostrated by the terrible blast that had swept the beautiful old garden, cutting down tree and shrub as level as if with a knife. Some of the men lay groaning where they had been cast, burned, wounded, and disfigured; while those who were uninjured, of whichever side, seemed as if by mutual consent to consider their petty strife at an end in the face of so awful a catastrophe, and, sheathing their swords, stood looking at the ruined house before them, confused and unmanned by the shock.

For to a man the explosion had so shaken them that a curious feeling of helplessness had succeeded to the energy they had displayed, and no one moved even to render assistance to the wounded.

Suddenly a loud voice shouted——

"Run, my lads, run! There will be another explosion directly. It is a plot to blow up the place."

This seemed to break the spell, and there was a rush of feet towards the closed bridge, when the founder's voice arose.

"No, no," he cried; "there can be no other explosion. It was my store; I thought it safe; the powder has all —— "

He stopped speaking, and reeled and nearly fell to the earth, for he had received a blow from a falling beam; but he recovered himself sufficiently to point towards the house in an appealing way that no one understood.

"Halt there!" cried Sir Mark, who now rose to his feet, from where he had been thrown, "follow me some of you, quick, before it is too late."

He might well add these last words, for, as the smoke rose like a heavy pall above the ruined house, it could be seen that, with the exception of a couple of the gables near where they stood, the place was shattered and nearly razed to the ground. There was a huge hole here, another cavernous rent there, and, piled above them, beams and rafters, blackened, smoking, and dotted with glowing embers, which began to sparkle as the portion of the house now standing burned furiously.

There was no need for light, for wood had entered largely into the construction of the building, and the powder seemed to have prepared everything to burn. With a rush great tongues of fire leaped from the embayment of the fine old parlour, whose diamond panes flew crackling out, while the lead in which they were set trickled down in a silvery stream. The whole of the parlour glowed in a few seconds like a furnace, and directly after the fire sprang forth from the two rooms above, and then again from the little window in the pointed gable, which was soon being licked from gutter to the copper vane on its summit by the orange and golden flames.

The rooms on either side rapidly followed, and soon the two gables that had remained after the explosion seemed wrapped in fire, which lit up the unscathed trees, and turned the lake as if into a pool of blood.

As Sir Mark sprang forward, a dozen men ran to his side—Gil's men, every one of them, for his own stood aloof; but as they went close up a rush of flame and smoke drove them back, scathing and scorching them so that it was impossible to face it.

"A ladder—a ladder—fetch a ladder!" cried Sir Mark.

The words were hardly uttered, before a couple of men picked up that which Wat Kilby had used as a weapon, and to which he still tightly clung, as he lay at some little distance, where he had been cast.

This was dragged from him, and a couple of men reared it, by Sir Mark's directions, against the burning casement of Mace's room.

Seizing the rounds Sir Mark climbed up, and reached the room, now all aglow, but as he felt the scorching flames, which were already burning the top of the short ladder, he rapidly descended and stood wringing his hands, while Gil's men seized poles, fetched buckets from a shed, and began to obtain water from the race.

" It is impossible!   My poor girl!   What shall I do ?" moaned Sir Mark.

Then to the men nearest he shouted, his voice sounding shrill and strange amidst the roar and flutter of the flames,

" There is a lady in yonder— a hundred golden pounds to the man who fetches her out."

There was a murmur amongst the little crowd, but no one stirred, and he repeated his offer.

" Are you men to stand there and see her burned to death ?" he cried.   " Two hundred pounds to the man who saves Mistress Mace Cobbe."

" D——n your two hundred pound," cried a hoarse voice, as a great gaunt blackened figure crawled into the glow.   " Up the ladder, my lads, there be two women there."

" Old Wat," cried the men, in a loud chorus of excitement, as the weird looking figure stretched out its hands, and seemed to grope blindly towards the ladder, but rolled down with a groan, utterly unable to make the attempt, having received some injury to the hip.

"Is there no man here who will try to save the helpless women?" cried Sir Mark. "That's right, my brave lad," he said, as one of Gil's men took a hatchet from his belt and ran up the burning ladder.

He seemed to beat back the flames with his hands, and bravely climbed in at the window, a roar of cheers following him, as he regularly leaped into the burning room. Then there was a shower of sparks, a rush of flame, and, to the horror of all present, the brave fellow was seen to literally roll out of the parlour casement, blackened and burned, having fallen at once through the floor to the room below.

"No one can be there and live," he gasped. "Water, boys, water! I am burn-ing: throw me in," he shrieked; and one of his companions deluged him with the contents of a bucket.

"It is all over. How horrible—how horrible!" groaned Sir Mark. "Quick lads, water, dash it in. Who is that?"

He started back almost in fear, as he saw Gil stride forward, pick up the fallen axe, and seize the ladder to drag it from the burning casement.

As he did so he staggered, for he was quite giddy yet from the blow he had received when the explosion cast him some twenty feet away; but he recovered directly, and, planting the ladder against the next window, he seemed to regain his strength, and dashed up axe in hand.

There was a lusty cheer at this, and Sir Mark gnashed his teeth, as he wondered why he had not thought of going up to the next window, where the flames seemed to burn less furiously, though the next instant they were pouring out from the shattered window beneath, and making the long trailing strands of roses and woodbine writhe and twine as if in agony, as the flames licked them up, and then seemed to wreathe themselves around the figure of Gilbert Carr.

With two vigorous blows, he dashed in the oaken divisions of the window, and as he struck the flames leaped into his face, wrapping round him; but he seemed to heed them not, for blow after blow fell, till he cleared the way, and then, leaving the burning ladder, he climbed right in, and a dead silence fell upon all present as he disappeared amidst the flames and smoke, which came rolling out more furiously than ever.

No man spoke for a while, as the fire crackled, and the tiles on the old house slipped, and fell rattling down. The copper vane suddenly began to burn in the intense heat with a vivid blue light like some firework. The ladder, which had stood out dark against the flaming windows, gradually burned till rounds and sides were so much glowing charcoal, and a dull sense of horror chilled to inaction the spectators of the gallant deed.

Suddenly Wat Kilby raised himself up on his knees, supporting his injured body with one hand, and lifting the other to wave above his head.

" His father's son!" he yelled, as the fire glistened in his wild eyes and blackened hairless face, for his grisly beard was scorched away—" his father's son — a Carr! — a Carr! —Culverin for ever! Fetch him out brave boys—a rescue—a rescue! Forward boys— Board!"

As he yelled out these words, they seemed to electrify his followers, and with a shout the crew dashed to the burning house as if about to plunge in.

There was no hesitation now, not a man flinched, but, leaping in through the lower burning window, the ladder fell in so many glowing fragments amidst the feet of the foremost, who disappeared for a few brief moments, and then re-appeared with Gil Carr, bearing out through the flames a figure that seemed to be clad in gold, so glistening and yellow seemed the satin dress, with its stomacher of pearls.

The men drew back from him as Gil bore his burden on towards what had once been the shady lawn of the garden, and laid it reverently down, tearing a handkerchief from his breast to cover the ghastly mutilation of the face, and then crushing out as he knelt the smouldering flames and sparks that had attacked the wedding-dress.

"Mace, my darling!" cried Sir Mark, passionately.

"Back!" cried Gil, fiercely; "touch her not, upon your life."

Sir Mark shrank away, appalled by the fierce gaze of the man who knelt there upon one knee, reverently arranging the garments

round the dead, whom he had found com-
paratively untouched by the flames, but
pinioned and crushed by a fallen beam. He
heeded not his own sufferings, though those
who stood by could see that the doublet he
wore was falling from his breast in pieces;
that the leather of his belt and boots had
crumpled up in the intense heat; and that
his hands and face were horribly scorched.

"Let me see her, let me see her," cried a
harsh voice, and the little crowd parted to
let Wat Kilby crawl forward. "Is it Janet?
Tell me, brave boys, is it my lass? The
cursed powder has taken away my sight.
Tell me, brave boys, is it my little, bright,
tricksy Janet?"

"No, no, no," moaned a piteous voice;
"it is my child—my darling child. Oh,
Mace, Mace, joy of my poor old heart, has
it come to this?"

There was so piteous an appeal in these
words—so intense, so terrible was the suf-

fering they betokened—that the men drew back as the founder staggered to the side of the dead, let himself fall upon his knees, and there crouched with his hands clasped together in his lap, gazing helplessly down.

The remains of the Pool-house burned brightly still; the flames licked up rafter and beam; the red-hot tiles cracked and splintered and fell with a crash from time to time, sending up a whirlwind of sparks; and the blaze that lit up the Pool and forest far and near made plain, as if seen by day, the piteous group on the old lawn. But no one heeded the fire now, or dreamed of there being danger of the flying embers setting light to one or other of the powder sheds. Every thought was turned to the bereaved father; and as Sir Mark stood there, among his followers and the workpeople, one of the few unscathed by the fire, he found himself, bridegroom-elect although he had been, a person apparently of very secondary import, for next to Jeremiah Cobbe men and women gazed upon Gil Carr.

Just then the founder raised one of his trembling hands and stretched it out to reach the kerchief Gil had so lovingly placed over the mutilated face, but the latter stayed him.

"No, no," he said in a low voice, "for your own sake no. Let us remember our darling as she was."

The old man's hand closed upon the scorched palm, and then he laid the other upon it and held it, gazing piteously in the other's face.

"Right, Gil," he said in a cracked voice. "Right! Let us remember *our* darling as she was."

There was a pause here, and a beam fell in the burning house, causing a whirlwind of sparks to rise.

"Forgive me, Gil," continued the founder. "Even if this hand did slay Abel Churr, the fire has purged it. Brave boy—brave boy! I was very hard on both!"

"Over her who lies here I swear I am innocent of that man's blood," said Gil softly; and then in a lower tone, "My darling—my darling—you believed my words."

"And so do I, Gil," cried the old man piteously. "Oh, my child, my child! God in heaven, how have I sinned that I should suffer this?"

A shudder ran through the crowd, so wild and piercing suddenly rose the old man's upbraiding cry, while like an echo to his words came a shrill, harsh voice from the direction of the ruins, where, on a heap of smouldering wood and stones, stood Mother Goodhugh, like a black silhouette against the flames.

"Woe to the wicked house! Woe to the maker of deadly grains! Woe to the caster of cannon and culverin and gun!"

There was a dead silence, and then, amidst

the crackling of the blazing wood and the fluttering of the flames, rose once more the voice of Mother Goodhugh, as she gesticulated and waved her stick.

"What did I say? What did I foretell against this evil man and his house? Did I not cry, it was cursed, and that the curse would fall? Look at the wicked place! And now once more I raise up my voice, and tell thee that a curse will fall on him or her who touches stick or stone to try and raise it up again. Let it burn—let it be level with the earth, and become a refuge for snakes and toads and unclean things. Let no man try to build it up, or be he cursed as well."

"Silence, hag!" cried Sir Mark passionately.

"Nay," she cried, "I will not hold my peace. Go thou, young man, and rejoice that thou art saved from to-morrow—saved from wedding to the daughter of one whom

I had cursed. Who doubts the power of Mother Goodhugh now? Speak, Jeremiah Cobbe, did I not foretell the ruin of thy house?"

"My poor child. My little love—where are thy pretty sayings now, where thy prattling ways? Little Mace—pretty little Mace! How old is she to-day, mother?" said the founder, gazing at vacancy, with a smile, for the old woman's words had not reached his ears. "Six, eh? six. Why what a great age for my darling to have grown. Gil, my boy, God bless thee, lad! You have grown stout and well again, and I look to thee to protect my little one from harm. There, you must love her; take thy little sister; keep her from the pool, and mind her pretty little feet don't stray near the water side. Hey, boy, did'st ever see such bonny little feet, so white and pink, and pretty, it seems a sin to put them into leather shoes. Be good to her, my brave stout lad, and some day—who knows ?—thou may'st perhaps like to make her thy own little wife. If thou dost, ha, ha, ha! she shall not disgrace thee, boy, for she shall be a very lady in her way."

He looked round with a vacant smile, and nodded pleasantly at Gil.

" Cursed ! I tell thee—cursed ! " cried Mother Goodhugh. "It has been a long time coming, but it has come at length. Look how it smokes and burns. Didst hear the noise the devilish powder made ? Ha ! ha ! ha ! That which he made to destroy others has destroyed himself. Burn, flames, burn ! " she cried, waving her stick ; " burn wood and stones, and burn until all is level with the dust ! "

The crowd stood round her at a respectful distance listening to her ravings, and had she been the wise woman she professed to be, she would have known where to stop and beat a hasty retreat, with a great increase, among the simple people, to her reputation. But it was not to be.

Just then, borne in a lumbering carriage that this time had braved all the ruts, up came Sir Thomas Beckley, with Mistress Anne and Master Peasegood.

The old woman caught sight of Anne Beckley as she descended hastily from the carriage, and approached her with a malicious, triumphant look.

Just then the jealous girl caught sight of the prostrate body in its wedding dress, and seemed petrified.

"What did I say—what did I say?" cried a voice behind her, and turning she encountered Mother Goodhugh's malignant eyes.

This was too much for Anne, who crept shuddering away, when the burning house, the kneeling figure by the dead, the whole scene seemed to swim round her, and she would have fallen but for Sir Mark, who caught her in his arms.

"Oh, it is too dreadful—too dreadful!" she murmured, and closed her eyes.

"Master Peasegood, will you take him to your house?" said Gil. "Poor soul! the shock has been too heavy for his brain."

"Eh! Go with Master Peasegood? Yes," said the founder smiling. "Gil, brave lad, you'll see that my darling does not come to harm."

Gil bowed his head, and as the founder rose from his knees smiling and ready to accompany the parson, down whose cheeks the great tears coursed, Mother Goodhugh climbed on a heap of stones, waving her hands wildly as she saw her enemy pass.

"Woe to him; woe to his house!" she shrieked excitedly.

"Silence that vile witch's mouth," cried Sir Thomas.

"A witch, a witch!" cried a voice; and Wat Kilby, who had dragged himself up once more upon his hands and knees, waved one hand again towards the burning ruins, which had just burst forth into fiercer flames.

"A witch—a witch!" he yelled, "away with her, and let her burn."

A shout rose from Sir Mark's followers, and, with a rush, they surrounded the old woman, who struck at them with her stick as she was seized. Then, in spite of her shrieks and appeals, she was borne towards the burning ruins.

The burning of a witch was so congenial an occupation, that, failing a great triumph over Gil Carr's crew, the followers of Sir Mark took to their task with such gusto that in another minute Mother Goodhugh would have been hurled into the flames.

It was in Anne Beckley's power to save her by a quick appeal to Sir Mark; but she hesitated, for the thought flashed across her mind that, Mother Goodhugh dead, she would carry with her many secrets, and, above all, the greatest one, of how this terrible affair had been brought about. It might have been accident; but she had her doubts.

Sir Thomas looked on in puzzled guise. He knew he ought to do or say something, but without his clerk he was generally at sea, while Master Peasegood, who might have given him good advice, had gone off, leading the stricken father to his home.

It was Gil who interfered, and none too soon.

Springing up from where he had knelt on one knee, he threw himself before the would-be executioners.

"Shame on you!" he cried; and the men stopped short, while Mother Good-hugh struggled from them to throw herself on the earth and cling to Gil's knees.

"Save, oh, save me!" she shrieked; "I cannot die."

"What are you, that you interfere?" cried one of the men.

"A witch—a witch—to the flames," cried Wat Kilby, in his harsh voice.

"Silence, old dog!" roared Gil.

"In with her, lads!" cried the first of the men, seizing Mother Goodhugh by the shoulder; but, as she shrieked with horror, the man went down from a blow given by Gil's clenched hand, which the next moment sought his sword, to find it gone.

With a shout, the others closed round Gil, but this roused his own followers, who ran up and dragged Mother Goodhugh away. They faced Sir Mark's men, and, weapons being drawn, there was an imminent risk of a renewal of the fight, when Sir Thomas's fat voice was heard, sounding weak and tremulous, for the baronet was terribly alarmed.

"Stop! my good men," he cried; "you must not burn her until she has been tried. A woman suspected of witchcraft must—er —er—must—er—er—be taken before—er—

er—the nearest justice of the peace—er—er
—er—that is me, you see, and——"

" Escape without a word," whispered Gil
to the old woman. " I'll cover your flight."

" Bless thee for ——"

" Keep thy blessings and thy curses," said
Gil, sternly. " Go."

Mother Goodhugh shrank trembling away,
the village people and the workers opening
to let her pass, while, when Sir Mark's men
advanced to try and retake her, they were
met by the swords of Gil's crew.

" Don't; pray don't let them fight,"
whispered Anne in agony.

" Is this a seemly time for a fresh encounter,
Sir Mark?" said Gil.

" Not if you give yourself up," was the reply.

" I give up—to you?" said Gil. " Let who
interferes with me and my men do so at
his peril. This way, my lads," he cried.
" There is a cloak behind yon shed. It was
meant for thee, sweet," he whispered, as he

bent down over the dead, "to keep thee from the cold;" and upon its being brought the lifeless figure, in its wedding-dress, was reverently lifted and borne into Tom Croftly's house.

Sir Mark concluded to engage in no further encounter that night, telling himself that he could easily take Gil another time. So, calling off his men, he allowed him to superintend the removing of the lifeless girl, Anne Beckley now following trembling into the cottage, awe-stricken as she was at being in the presence of death, while, when at last day broke and the bright sun rose, it was upon a heap of ashes smouldering and smoking still. Where the pleasant old garden had been alive with verdure, teeming fruit-trees, and autumn flowers, was a space of trampled blackened soil, while for fifty yards round the trees had been scorched and stripped not only of their leaves, but of every minor twig and spray.

Sir Mark scowled angrily again and again at Gil, and his men gave the sailors many a menacing look, as they took upon themselves the duty of keeping watch by the house where the poor girl lay.

It was Gil's men, too, who tried to search the ashes of the Gabled House for the remains of poor Janet, the only other occupant of the building; but the task was given up, on its being found that the intense heat had fused metal, and reduced the stones so that they crumbled at the touch.

CHAPTER VII.

HOW MASTER PEASEGOOD PREACHED WISDOM.

GIL's ship, with Father Brisdone on board, after waiting in vain for its freight, grounded as the tide went down. The old priest, who had been on deck, leaning over the bulwarks gazing up the river for the boat that did not come, had been startled by a great flash of light which suddenly shot up above the hills, and then by a heavy clap as of thunder, followed shortly by a fierce glow in the sky, all of which told him only too plainly of some terrible catastrophe at the powder-works.

He was not surprised, then, that the boat did not arrive till the long, weary night had passed away, and the bright sun shone once more upon the dancing waters, but even then noon was fast approaching before there was the measured dip of oars, and the boat came round a wooded point.

He looked earnestly for Mace, but, not seeing her, he sighed.

" My eyes fail me a good deal now," he said ; and, shading them with his hand, he stood watching till, as the boat neared the ship, he could see that she had four men lying in the stern sheets, and he concluded that there had been an encounter.

" A bad augur," he said, sadly ; " blood-shed on the eve of a wedding. Poor boy though, there seems no chance of a wedding, for he has not won his love."

His hands trembled as he stood at the gangway, while the boat was run up to the side and Gil painfully climbed on board.

" Failed, my son?" cried Father Brisdone and here he stopped short as he saw the terrible look of anguish in the young man's eyes.

" Help my poor lads, father," he said sadly. " They have been lying hurt these many hours."

One by one four injured men were hoisted on board, and laid beneath the shelter of a sail, while Gil and the father attended to their injuries with rough but sensible surgery. There was a severe sword-wound and plenty of terrible burns, but the worst sufferer was poor Wat Kilby, whose face was blackened by the explosion, hair and beard burned off, and his thigh-bone broken.

He was in a high fever and wandering when slung on board, turning angrily upon those who had helped him.

" Don't I tell you the poor lass is burning ? " he cried. " This is your doing, skipper," he moaned. " You were always against it, and now you leave the poor lass to burn, and keep me here. Father, this is the boy I watched over and brought up, and taught. This be the way he treats me now I am in trouble."

It was with great difficulty that they could keep the poor old fellow sufficiently quiet to enable them to perform the necessary bandaging, but at last he sank into the heavy sleep of exhaustion; and Gil, having satisfied himself that his injured men were cared for, saw to his own burns, gave orders for the ship to be floated up to her old berth on the next tide, and then returned to the Pool.

For the next seven days he was almost constantly at Roehurst, in company with the stricken father, whom affliction seemed to have turned back to him as his only friend; and together they hung about the ruins, which still smouldered slightly, and crumbled more and more into a shapeless heap, overhung by a few masses of tottering wall.

Gil would have tried to persuade the old

man to leave the spot, but that it had so terrible a fascination for him as well, and together they would sit hour after hour gazing at the ruins, and rebuilding the place mentally and occupying it as of old.

The people of the sparsely inhabited district came to gaze at the wreck, and from far and near they gathered together two days after the fire, to see Gil's men carry the flower-sprinkled bier from Croftly's house to the little rustic churchyard two miles away, the men taking it in turns to bear her, four and four about. The place was densely crowded, thinly populated as was the country there, to see Gil Carr and the weak, broken founder, who seemed to have aged in one night to a venerable old man, walk hand in hand behind, and stand bareheaded while Master Peasegood read, and sobbed, and read, and finally letting fall his book, went down upon his knees in the soft earth, and prayed beside the grave.

Sir Mark chafed more and more, but it was in vain. He was to have been chief actor in another scene; here he was completely set aside again, and Gil Carr had resumed his place.

Fortunately for Sir Mark, his old acquaintance Sir Thomas Beckley came forward to offer his hospitality, and he took up his abode with him, feeling that he could not leave the place with his task undone, and in a bitter mood he received the attempts at consolation offered to him by Anne, who, however, always kept very much aloof, playing the part of the injured woman, but promising herself a sharp revenge, if ever the King's messenger should again lay siege unto her heart.

Up to the day of the funeral the founder had been almost childish from the effects of the shock; but after that he seemed to have recovered himself, though he looked aged and bent, and changed to a remarkable degree.

"I was very hard upon you, Gil," he said to him one evening, as they stood leaning against one of the posts that had helped to support the swing bridge now completely swept away, and whose place was occupied by a couple of stout planks laid across the race. "I was very hard upon you, my lad, but, though I made that affair of Abel Churr's an excuse, I don't think I believed at heart that you did away with the poor wandering wretch."

Gil looked at him sadly, and bowed his head without speaking.

"What are you going to do now, my lad?" continued the founder, gazing at him with a yearning look as one his lost child had loved.

"To do?" said Gil, in a low hopeless tone, "to do? What is there left to do, sir, but die?"

"Hush, my lad," said the founder, laying a trembling hand upon the young man's arm; "that is for me to say. I am old and stricken: the storm has torn one great branch from the trunk, and the old tree will slowly wither and die. You are young yet, and hope will come to you again as time goes on."

"Hush, for God's sake, hush!" cried Gil, turning upon him almost fiercely; then, gazing round him in the gathering gloom of the evening, he let himself sink upon his knees lower and lower, with his hands covering his face, as for the first time in the solitude of that blasted home he gave full vent to the pent-up agony that for days and days he had striven to hide.

"Hope," he groaned, "hope?" as his broad shoulders heaved and the despairing sobs tore their way from his weary breast. "He does not know what she was to me— he cannot tell how I loved her. Mace, Mace, my darling, would to God I were lying by thy side!"

It had grown quite dark now, and the founder sank upon his knees in the black ashes to lay his hands upon the young man's head.

"Gil, my son," he whispered hoarsely, "forgive me, for I never knew your heart till now. In her name I ask you to forgive me for the wrong I would have done you both in tearing you apart. I thought I was doing right, but I am punished for my fault."

"Forgive you!" groaned Gil, who, for the first time in his life, was quite unmanned. "Yes, I forgive you, if there is aught to forgive."

He pressed the old man's hand, as he rose after a time, weak and desolate, to sit down upon one of the stones cast from the main building by the blast. Some distance away a couple of windows shed their feeble light, as if they were signals to Mace to open her casement once again, and a groan rose to

Gil's lips as he thought of the past. Then, like a wandering spirit, a white, filmy-looking owl swept by them, turned and came back once more, as if attracted by the blackened ruins, glided to and fro for a few minutes, and it seemed to the two men that it shrieked faintly just over the very centre of the ruined house before it glided away.

Gil sat watching the bird in a dreamy, hopeless way, and, as he gazed through the darkness, he felt that the place would become the home of such creatures.

He was aroused from his reverie by the founder.

"How did it happen, Gil?" he said.

He spoke in a low, hoarse voice, but his words sounded very plain in the silence of the autumn even.

"How did it happen?" said Gil, repeating his words.

"Yes, my boy, tell me all. I cannot believe that God would make that old woman

with her curses his instrument to punish
me."

"I have little to tell," said Gil. "I saw
our darling again and again, begging that
she would go with me; but she refused till
she found it hopeless to move you, and that
the wedding was to be."

"Yes, yes—go on," groaned the founder.

"Then she consented, and I made my
plans."

"Yes, I see," replied the founder, "you
were there with your men, and Sir Mark
felt sure that you were coming. But yours
was a mad revenge on him, and meant ruin
and destruction to all."

"I do not understand you," said Gil,
quietly.

"Did you think by blowing down part of
the place to get her away in the confusion?"

"Blow down? The place?" said Gil.
"We had not a charge of powder with us. I
left it all on board."

" Then it was the store below caught first," said the founder, musingly; "but how —how ?"

" I cannot tell," said Gil.

" Wat Kilby," exclaimed the founder, jumping at a cause for the terrible disaster; "he was smoking his tobacco by the entry, and must have thrown down the burning pipe."

" Nay, he did not smoke; he was by my side bearing a ladder."

" Are you speaking frankly to me, Gil?" said the founder. " I prithee keep nothing back."

" Can you speak to me like that ?" replied Gil, in a grave, reproachful tone. " Master Cobbe, I have kept nothing back; I have added nothing to my story; I have only left out that there was the priest awaiting on board of my ship, to be our darling's companion until we were made man and wife."

" Forgive me, Gil," said the founder. " I

know now that you are keeping nothing back.   But how could it have happened ?"

"A shot from one of Sir Mark's men's pieces must have gone through to your store of powder," said Gil.   "They did fire, but my men struck their pieces aside."

The founder accepted this theory, and they sat in silence for a few moments, till they were interrupted by the approach of a great, dark figure, who seemed at last to make them out.

"Ah ! friend Cobbe," it said, in the thick rich tones of Master Peasegood, "I was seeking thee.   Come ; the night-dew is falling, and it is time you were safely housed. Ah ! Gil, my good lad, you here ?"

"Yes," was the curt response.   "Master Peasegood, hadst thou but done thy duty by her who was thy charge, these troubles might not have been."

"Reproach me not, good lad, I was taken away through Sir Mark's scurvy tricks and carried up to London. And there I was, day after day, half prisoner, half free. Sometimes they'd let me fly a little bit, like a bird with a string at its leg. Other times they'd keep me in, and never a word could I get to know of my offence."

" Not a legal prisoner, then ? "

" Nay, lad, not at all. Though, had I tried to flee I had been tied fast enough, I'll warrant. I took advantage of my freedom to see St. Paul's, and should be sorry to preach there. I bought me though, as I had my money with me and the chance was good, six yards of cloth in Paul's churchyard to make me a goodly cloak—four pounds sixteen it cost me—and seven yards of calamanko for a cassock ; one pound four and sixpence that, besides a pound for a new hat, and six shillings for a lutestring hood for Mistress Hilberry. I lightened my pocket, Gil, but I was heavy enough at heart."

Gil nodded.

" I grew so hot of blood and angry at last with the way they kept me in, and the too free use I made of the most villainous ale, Master Cobbe, I ever put to my lips, that had I not been blooded freely by a chirurgeon, I should have been ill. It was not the proper time — the hæmeroyal time, though close upon the full, but I let him take a good ten ounces from my veins, and felt a better man."

" It would have been better, Master Peasegood, had you been here."

" True, lad, but I was not my own ruler. That Sir Mark never trusted me. I had hard work to get free again, and hurried down to get to our darling's side. You saw me when I came—that night ? Sir Thomas Beckley overtook me, and he brought me on."

Gil bent his head, and held out his hand, which the other pressed.

"When do you sail again?" said the parson.

"I sail again? Maybe never," said Gil. "Why should I sail?"

"To give thyself occupation—work—toil-weary evening and restful night. Up, man, and work. Bear thy load bravely till Heaven send the soft touch of time to make it lighter. Thou art young; thy ship waits. Go across the sea and do thy work. This is no place for thee."

"Why do you interfere with me, Master Peasegood?" cried Gil, testily. "I am none of thy followers."

"Nay, my lad, thou art not; but I give thee good advice that my lips seemed urged to speak. Go and toil, and sit not down sobbing like a fretful child."

"Man, you would madden me if I listened," cried Gil.

"Nay, but thou shalt listen," said Master Peasegood, "and I will quell thy madness.

Thou hast received one terrible loss like a man; I would not have thee do it like a woman. Then, too, Master Cobbe, when are these fires to be relit, and the wreathing curls of smoke to rise from each furnace chimney?"

"Never," said the founder sadly, "my energy has gone, and I am spent."

"Tut, tut, man; fie!"

"What have I to live for?" cried the founder, as angry now as Gil.

"Not for thyself," cried Master Pease-good. "Not both of ye to indulge a moping selfish regret, but for others—for the memory of one dead. Tut! man, those do not pay most respect to their dead who sit and sigh, and groan, and work themselves into fevers. Gil Carr, thy men call for thee to lead them in some seafaring adventure. Jeremiah Cobbe, thou hast got together here some fifty souls —workmen, their wives, and the children they have begotten. Thou didst bring them to do thy work, and now the furnaces are cold, the busy wheel has ceased to turn, and thy workmen lean against the doorposts, and idle, and get out of trim. Come, come! up, and be doing."

"For whom?" cried the founder angrily, "for whom should I toil?"

"Not for thyself, but for thy people. Nay, nay! don't take it ill, and think me unfeeling. To both of you I say it is your duty, and, in the name of yon sweet girl whom we all so dearly loved, I say keep her memory green in your heart of hearts, but cease unmanly repinings against fate."

"Ah! Master Peasegood," said the founder more gently, "thou hast never been a father."

"Had I been sweet Mace's father could I have loved her better, Jeremiah Cobbe? Have not mine eyes oft filled with tears at the memory of her sweet face; has not my voice choked, and have not my words failed when I have tried to speak, Gil Carr? Tut, man, give me credit for loving her as well. Thou hast felt sore against me because I tried to keep you two apart; but why was it, Gil, why was it? Had I not seen that which made me think thou would'st prove a faithless lover to her, poor child. Give me your hand, man, my love for her was different to thine, but it was quite as deep."

Gil's hand was laid in the heavy palm of the parson of Roehurst, and they joined in a close firm grip without another word.

" When shall these fires be going again, Master Cobbe," continued the parson; "when shall the busy wheel turn plashing round? Come, come, promise me that thy mourning shall not be quite out of bounds."

The founder had turned his back, and remained gazing away from them at the blackened heap.

" You will be up and doing, will you not, Master Cobbe?" continued the parson, urging him on. "Come: for thy child's sake. Would'st have this place left a ruin? Come, promise me thou wilt."

A deep sigh seemed to tear itself from the founder's breast, and he turned to gaze in the direction of his works.

"Thou art right, parson," he said; "it is not fair that the workmen I brought here to feed and furnish with hard labour should suffer for my sake. The fires shall be lit again."

"Ay, that's well," said Master Peasegood earnestly. "It will be glad news for many a heart. Then I shall see the axe busy again as the leaves fall, and the glow of the charcoal fire in the woods; and meantime thy men will delve for iron, and the furnaces go roaring on. Is it not so?"

"Yes."

"Bravely spoken, brave heart," said Master Peasegood; "and thou, Gil Carr, off to thy ship once more, and bear away her freight. Come back to us laden with the pale yellow brimstone and the grey-white salt. Tut, tut, tut, of what am I speaking?" he muttered, as Gil shuddered. "You will go, my brave lad, eh?"

"I suppose so: yes," said Gil slowly; and the parson laid his hand upon the founder's shoulder once more.

"And the dear old house, Master Cobbe? There is sandstone waiting in the quarry to be borne here, and thou hast oaken timber enough cut to build it up. When wilt begin to repair thy loss?"

"Never," cried the founder fiercely. "Parson Peasegood, I'll work and toil and invent and strive day and night to keep things going here, but it is for others' sake, not mine."

"Nay, nay, but the house must be restored."

"Never," cried the founder; "never, Master Peasegood; never, Gil Carr. I care nothing for the words of that reviling old woman and her curses. Punishments come from Heaven, not from Hell, and, if she be a witch, 'tis devil's work she does ; but no hand shall touch yon heap, neither stone nor ash shall be disturbed. The flowers may spring up again, and the grass will grow, but to touch it would be to me like disturbing my poor child's grave. Our dear old home died with my darling. Let them rest."

He turned away and walked firmly across the planks towards the lane where Tom Croftly's cottage stood, followed by the parson and Gil, who stepped back as the founder rapped upon the cottage door.

" Tom," he said, as the door was opened, and the light of a rush candle shone upon his deeply-lined face, " go round to the men and bid them light the big furnace in the morning, and you see about the mixing up of another batch of powder."

" Hurray, master," cried the man. " Give me my hat, wife. Dal me! but that's good news again."

" Thou'lt go on making powder again—so soon ? " said Master Peasegood, as the founder joined them, and they went down the lane.

" Yes," said the founder firmly. " Gil, when thou com'st back, my lad, there will be some score barrels of the best and strongest make. I want to show people that an old hag's curses are as light as wind."

" Ay, and that a bad mishap is not to be taken as a judgment, because a would-be soothsayer says 'tis so," cried Master Peasegood. " Thou'rt right, Master Cobbe. I thank Heaven I spoke to you both as bravely as I did, for my heart misgave me all the while."

The next morning the smoke rolled up once more from the furnace chimney. The great wheel turned and plashed as it shed showers of silver from its broad paddles and spokes; blackened men bore baskets of soft dogwood charcoal to be ground, and others shovelled up the pale yellow sulphur and the crystals of potash for mixing into powder once again. Two heavy tumbrils jolted and blundered down the cinder-made lane to fetch great loads of ironstone from the pits in the woods whence it was dug, and then fierce furnaces were charged with layers of ore and charcoal ready for smelting, while the horses tugged at their loads in answer to the uncouth cries of the men. It was as if the people of Roehurst had awakened from sleep, and all were rejoicing in the gladsome feeling of being once more at work after their enforced idleness, the change acting like a spur. There was shouting over the various works, and now and then some one burst forth into a song, some doleful love-ditty about a sweet young maiden, sung in a minor key.

Tom Croftly was in his element once
more, and after seeing the furnaces started
and the men preparing the next batch of
powder, he anxiously set his colliers to work
to get him more coal.

It was no sending down a set of blackened
miners with their Davy lamps crowding a
cage that dropped slowly into the gas and
choke-damp charged bowels of the earth,
but the superintending of couples of men
who attacked some cords of wood—long,
low stackings of the loppings of the trees
cut down the previous winter—and, clearing
out a circular space, throwing out the earth
all round, they set up a pole in the centre.
Then picking the branches that were some
four feet long, they carefully began to build
them round the centre pole, standing all on
end, and going on round and round till a low
circular stack was built, when the stout
central pole was taken away, the space it
occupied being filled with light brushwood,

which was then set alight ready to communicate with the wood around, while the
air runing in through spaces left at the sides
soon made a swift fire. This, however, was
not allowed to burn fiercely, for old charcoal powder mixed with dry earth lay ready,
and, after the stack had been covered with
a litter of weeds, dry grass, and thin twigs
from the fallen trees sufficient to keep it
from falling through, the earth was shovelled
on all over the stack wherever there was a
sign of flame or thin smoke breaking
forth, till at last the flames were stifled
and the thick smoke rose only from the
centre.

"More loam on," cried Tom Croftly,
who, spade in hand, danced excitedly round
the charcoal pile like a grim black demon
busy over some fiery task, and the men
worked and watched, smothering the flames
with more earth and water till not a gleam
was seen, though all the while the fire was

glowing fiercely and burning out the watery gases of the wood.

And this went on night and day, the colliers having a shelter rigged up to keep off the night-air when they needed rest, this being called turn and turn, for, should there be no one ready to throw on shovels-full of loam when the fire began to work a way through, the burning would be spoiled.

But there were no burnings spoiled with Tom Croftly, who, had the men been disposed to fail, would have been there to catch them lapsing and take the shovel in hand himself. So the charcoal burned its time, glowing slowly in the well-closed heat till by gentle testing here and there it was declared to be quite fit, when the earth was cleared away, water used liberally for quenching, and the erst flaming heap allowed to cool, the effect being that the branches of rough wood were turned into black clinking metallic-sounding charcoal, hard and brittle to the touch, and ready to fuse the ironstone or turn into potent powder in the mill.

Then by slow degrees the traces of the explosion were softened down, and a new bridge took the place of that which had been swept away. A fresh fence, too, was made of riven oak, and surrounded the ruined garden, so that Master Peasegood had hopes that the founder had re-considered his words.

But he had not. The fence was there to protect the ruins from the feet of straying cattle. It was not needed to keep off the people of the little place, for they gazed upon it with awe, and whispered that it was haunted by the dead. And, when Master Peasegood asked thereof, the founder said his words stood firm. But this was when weeks had glided by, and Gil Carr's ship was tossing far away upon the sea.

CHAPTER VIII.

HOW THE BECKLEY PULLET RULED THE ROOST.

DAME BECKLEY was one of the happiest women under the sun, for she had scarcely a care. Her sole idea of home management was obedience, and she obeyed her lord implicitly. Next to him she yielded no little show of duty to her daughter, who ruled her with a rod of iron, which she changed for one of steel when dealing with her father.

"Well, my dear," said the dame, "speaking as a woman of the world, I must say I think it hardly becoming of us to keep Sir Mark here after his behaviour to us before. See how he slighted us. Fancy a man who calls himself a courtier telling a lady of title that her camomile tea that she has made with her own hands—it was the number one, my dear, flavoured with balm—was no better than poison."

"Never mind the camomile tea, mother. I tell you I wish Sir Mark to be persuaded to stay."

"Ah, well, my dear, if you wish it, of course he shall be pressed. I'll tell him that you insisted —"

"Mother!"

"La! my dear, what have I done now?" cried Dame Beckley. "You quite startle me when you stamp your feet and look like that."

"How can you be so foolish, mother? Go—go, and tell Sir Mark—insist upon his staying here."

"Well, my dear, and very proud he ought to be, I'm sure. Why, when I was young, if a gentleman had——"

"Mother!"

"There, there, my dear, I've done. I'll try and persuade Sir Mark to stay. I'm sure it would do him good, though I don't want him. It always seems to me that that terrible explosion sent a regular jar through what Master Furton, the Queen's chirurgeon, called the absorbens. If he were my son, I should certainly make him take a spoonful of my conserve of elder night and morning, and drink agrimony tea three times a day. In cases where there is the slightest touch of fever there is nothing—bless the girl, why she has gone, when did she go out of the room?"

Mistress Anne had gone away directly after her last imperious utterance of the word "mother," and walked straight to her father's room.

She had left Dame Beckley busy over her herbal, and she now found her father also on

study bent, his book being a kind of magis-
trates' *vade mecum* of those days on the
subject of witchcraft, and the author his
Majesty the King.

"What are you reading, father?" she
said, making him start as she came suddenly
behind him and laid her hand upon his
shoulder.

"His Majesty's book, my dear."

"Why?"

"Well, you see, my dear, it behoves me
as a justice of the peace to be well informed
of his Majesty's views respecting the heinous
sin of witchcraft, and to know how I should
comport myself and deal with so foul a
creature in case, at any future time ——"

"Mother Goodhugh should be brought
before you?"

"Yes, exactly," said the baronet. "My
dear Anne, I'd give almost everything I
possess for your clear discerning head."

"Never mind my head, father," she said,

with a half-laugh; "I want to speak to you about more important things."

"Yes, my dear, certainly. But won't you sit down? You worry me when you tower over me so, and threaten, and preach at me. Do sit down, child, pray."

"Nay, father, you can hear what I have to say without my seating myself."

"Yes, my dear," said Sir Thomas, humbly.

"Let Mother Goodhugh be, father."

"But, my child, she is a most pestiferous witch."

"For the present, father. For the present, let her be."

"Well, my dear, if you wish it, of course —— "

"I do wish it, father."

"How odd, my dear, that you should come to say that, when I was studying up the matter."

"I did not come to say that, father," said

Anne; "but to speak to you about our guest."

"Yes, my dear, he has been here now six weeks since that disaster."

"Seven weeks, father."

"Well, my child, seven weeks if you like; and he has sent back those soldier fellows and his own attendants, and seems to have settled himself down. I mean to tell him that he had better —— "

"Stay here till his health is quite recovered, father."

"Nay, indeed, my child, after his grossly neglectful behaviour to us, I feel ready at any time to send him away."

"But you will do no such thing, father. Sir Mark is your guest, and an important officer of his Majesty."

"An' if he had not been I should very soon —— "

"Your good treatment of so important a gentleman may mean something in the

future. It is always well, father, to have
friends at Court."

" Yes, yes, my child, but to leave us in so
scurvy a way, and take up his abode with
old Cobbe."

" That has nothing to do with the matter,
father.   Ask him to stay."

" But, Anne, my child."

" Father, I insist upon your forcing him
to stay."

" Force," said Sir Thomas ; " ah, there'll
be no need of that.   The job will be to
force him to go. But surely, child, thou'lt
never think of setting thy cap at him after
his engagement with the founder's child ? "

" I ? Set my cap ! Oh, father," she cried,
with a weak giggle, " that is too good.   I
absolutely hate him."

" Then I'll tell him we wish him——"

" To stay as long as he can, father.   Go
at once."

" But, my dear, he is going to-morrow.

He told me so when he was on his way to
the moat to fish, and I told him I was glad
to hear it."

" You told him that, father ? " cried Anne,
with flashing eyes.

" Indeed I did," said Sir Thomas.

" Then go at once," cried Anne, imperiously, "and bid him stay."

" But it will be like eating my words, my
child."

" Go eat them, then," cried the girl;
" and quickly. Say that you were but
jesting."

" And that you specially wished ——"

" No, father. Are you mad ? Say what
thou wilt, and canst; but mind this—Sir
Mark must stay."

Sir Thomas grumbled, but he had to go,
and he went, and very easily persuaded Sir
Mark to give up his project of leaving the
Moat next day, and so it came about that
about an hour later, when Mistress Anne was

wandering, book in hand, in the pleasaunce, beneath the sun-pleached trees, where the soft turf was dappled with sunshine and shade, she accidently came upon Sir Mark, moody and thoughtful, busy over his favourite occupation of trying to persuade one of the ancient carp in the moat to swallow a hook concealed in a lump of paste, a lure of which the said carp fought exceedingly shy.

If Sir Mark had been told a month before that he would become an angler—one of those patient beings who go and seat themselves on the banks of a piece of water and wait till a fish chooses to touch their bait— he would have laughed them to scorn.

All the same, though, he had gone to Sir Thomas Beckley's, very much shocked at the sudden termination of his matrimonial project, and had taken to his bed, where he stayed some days.

He told himself that he was heart-broken ; that he would never look upon woman's face again; that he would pay a pilgrimage yearly to Mace's grave, and live and die a heart-broken anchorite.

On the sixth day he arose and wrote a despatch concerning the state of Jeremiah Cobbe's manufactures, retiring certain proposals that he had made concerning the supply of guns and powder to his Majesty's forces. Later on he found that it would not be necessary to seize on Captain Carr, and later still followed the news that Gil had left those parts.

On the hearing of this he told himself that he could give full vent to his sorrow, which he did, taking at the same time a good deal of nutriment to counterbalance his sighs and tears.

Then, being a satisfactory moping pursuit for one so cut to the heart, he took to fishing week after week for the carp in the great moat; and after, on this particular day, trying in vain for one particularly heavy monster, he sighed very loudly—so loudly that it seemed to be echoed, and, looking sadly up, his eyes fell upon Mistress Anne, reading as she walked beneath the trees.

It was but a momentary glance, for she turned away directly after, and he sighed again, for he foresaw an interview with another lady as Dame Beckley came bustling to his side.

It was one way of showing his grief. A curious way of showing it; but every one has his peculiarities, and Sir Mark elected to dress himself more gorgeously than of old.

Sable had a prominent place in his costume, but it was largely relieved with gold lace and white linen, so that the angler who rose from his seat on the green bank of the old moat seemed, from the elegantly plumed hat to the shining rosetted shoes, more like one dressed for a ball or Court gathering than a man prepared to land the slippery carp or wriggling eel.

Dame Beckley was very nervous over her task, but she managed to acquit herself pretty well, and Sir Mark received her request that he should stay with a saddened smile that seemed to say all things were alike to him now.

" If my presence will give you pleasure, madam," he said with a sigh, " I will stay, though you will find me sorry company, I fear."

Sir Mark applied a delicate lace handker_ chief to his eyes, and spread around a faint odour of musk, before applying a fresh lump of paste to his great hook, and casting it once more between the water-lilies.

" Plague on the man," said Dame Beckley to herself ; " it is not a pleasure to me. I wish, though," she added musingly, "he would let me administer some of my simples. I could make him hearty and well."

Sir Mark sighed again when he was left

alone, and began to pity himself for his sufferings. Somehow he did not feel much sorrow for the young life that had been so suddenly cut off. His sorrow was for him who was to have been a bridegroom, and who would have succeeded to a goodly property with his handsome wife. This was the more important to him, as his little patrimony had been pretty well squandered, and his tailor was an extensive creditor who was eager to be paid.

"Yes," he said, "I'll stay. Poor woman, she wishes it, and, until my brain recovers from this dreadful shock, I am as well here as anywhere. Besides, I cannot well go back till I see my way to obtain some money."

Just then a great carp came slowly sailing along through the deep clear water, and rose amongst the stems of the water-lilies, as if to get a better glance with its big round eyes at the gorgeous object in black velvet, puffed with white satin and laced with gold, seated so patiently upon the bank.

" I begin to think now," said Sir Mark, as he gazed back at the carp, whose great round golden scales suggested coins, " that I have made a mistake. I might have had fair Mistress Anne."

The carp glanced down for a moment at the lump of paste, and shook its tail at it, its head being too rigid. The bait was not to its taste, so it rose higher and stared with its great round expressionless eyes, while it gasped with its big thick lips.

" Two hundred pounds for wedding garments of my own," he said, gazing back at the carp. " Twenty-five pounds for that new sword with the silver ornaments to the hilt, and five pounds for those white crane's plumes for my hat; and now they are useless. I cannot have them altered to wear now without spoiling them, and unless I marry soon that money is all thrown away."

He sighed again very softly, for he was exceedingly sorry for himself, as he thought of the founder's thousands.

"You are a lucky fellow," he continued, addressing the carp; "you always swim about clad in golden armour, and pay nothing for the show. True, I have not paid for mine, but I suppose that some day I shall be obliged."

Just then the carp smacked its lips as it thrust its nose above the water, gave its tail a lazy flap, and turned itself endwise so as to face Sir Mark, who gazed full at its fat gasping mouth, puffy eyes, and generally inane expression.

"What becomes of the old Beckleys?" said Sir Mark. "One might fancy that they all went to animate the bodies of the carp in this moat, for yon fish bears a wondrous resemblance to the baronet. I wonder whether he is as well clothed in golden scales. By all that's holy, here he is."

For, unnoticed on the soft velvety grass, Sir Thomas Beckley had come slowly up, looking in effect much more like the great carp than might have been considered possible, for his head was so charged with his daughter's mission that it seemed to force his mouth open, and his eyes from his head, while, as he came close up, he gasped two or three times, opening and shutting his lips without making a sound.

" Fishing, Sir Mark ? " he said at last, for want of something better to say. "You have captured one, I suppose ? "

"No, Sir Thomas," said his guest with a sigh. "Faith, an' I do not care to catch the poor things. I find in angling a change from dwelling on my sad thoughts. You never catch them, I suppose ? "

" No," was the reply, " I never do. My father once caught one."

" Indeed ! " said Sir Mark, yawning, for it was a peculiarity of Sir Thomas Beckley that he made everyone with whom he came into contact yawn.

" Yes," continued Sir Thomas. " It was during a very hot summer, and the moat was nearly dry. I remember it well."

" You seem to have an excellent recollection, Sir Thomas."

" I have, Sir Mark, I have," said the baronet pompously. " The great carp had somehow been left in a tiny pool whence he could not escape, so my father caught him."

" But not with a hook, Sir Thomas—he did not angle."

" Marry, sir, but he did. He'd have gone in after it but for the mud, which would have sullied his trunk hose and velvet breeches of murrey colour, so he had a kitchen meat hook tied to a long pole, and caught the big fish fairly."

"Indeed, Sir Thomas?   It must have been an exciting scene."

"My father was a great man, Sir Mark."

"Great and rich, Sir Thomas?"

"Very, Sir Mark."

"Then I have been doing wrong," thought Sir Mark. "This old idiot here must have inherited all the old man's money, unless ——-. Did your brothers much resemble him, Sir Thomas?" he said aloud.

"Brothers, sir?   I never had a brother. I was an only child."

"Indeed!   But I might have known. Sir Thomas, this is a fitting time to thank you for your hospitality. I may not have another chance before I go."

"But you will not go yet, Sir Mark.   I was about to press you to stay with us yet a while—till your health is more restored. You look pale and ill as yet, Sir Mark."

"Really, Sir Thomas?   Thanks for your

kindly concern, but I must go and try to recover elsewhere. Your good lady, Dame Beckley, has been trying to persuade me to stay, but I think my visit here has been too long already."

"Nay, nay," cried Sir Thomas, "we cannot spare you yet. You must think us very unfeeling if, after your terrible loss, you are not almost forced to stay here and recover. Not a word more, Sir Mark, not a word."

Sir Mark, however, endeavoured to put in several words, but was checked by his host, who left him afterwards, strutting away with a fat smile upon his countenance, and a belief in his heart that he had been doing some very hospitable act, Mistress Anne's commands being for the time entirely forgotten.

"That is settled then," said Sir Mark, as he kneaded a fresh piece of paste for the carp. "Perhaps in a few weeks I may find out some way of raising money, that is, when my heart has grown less sore."

He threw out his bait, and then settled himself with his back against a tree, to take a quiet nap, when, in a sheltered nook, where four huge hawthorns formed a kind of bower, he once more saw Mistress Anne busily reading, and, thinking that he ought to tell her of his intention to stay, he rose to saunter to her side.

CHAPTER IX.

HOW MASTER PEASEGOOD SAID HIS PRAYERS AND PAID A VISIT.

THERE was a deep, singular humming sound coming from the open window of Master Peasegood's cottage, and, as this noise passed through the big cherry-tree, it seemed to be broken up like a wind through a hedge, and to be somewhat softened. A stranger would not have known what it was, unless he had listened very attentively; and then he would have found that it was Master Peasegood saying his prayers.

" Sum — sum — sum — sum — sum — sum — sum—sum." It sounded like a gigantic bumble-bee. Then a few distinct words. Then

" sum — sum — sum — sum — sum," again; and you would hear, " Lead us not into temptation' — sum — sum — sum — especially with strong ales — sum — sum — sum — sum — sum — oh! Lord, I am so fleshly and so fat — sum — sum — sum — sum — I cannot do as I preach — sum — sum — sum — sum — I am a sadly hardened and weak man, oh! Lord — sum — sum — sum — sum; but I try to live at peace, and do to others as I would they should do unto me — sum — sum — sum — sum — Amen. Mistress Hilberry, I'm going out. Bring me my ale."

Master Peasegood was refreshed in mind, and proceeded to refresh himself in body, feeling at peace with the whole world, including Mother Goodhugh and all her works.

Mistress Hilberry came in, looking sour, but, as her eyes lit on the jovial face before her, some of its amiability was reflected back upon her own; and, finally, as the stout parson drank up his great jug of ale with the heartiest of enjoyment, she almost smiled.

"How thou dost take to thy ale!" she said.

"Ay, how naturally we do take to all bad habits, Mistress Hilberry; but a man cannot be perfect, and the possession of one wicked little devil may keep out seven devils, all much worse. I don't think it would be right to be quite good, Mistress Hilberry, so I take my ale."

"If thou never take nothing worse, master," said Mistress Hilberry—who was in a good temper—"thou wilt do;" and she seized the empty vessel and went out.

"Hah!" sighed Master Peasegood, taking his pipe off the mantel-piece, and looking at it ruefully, "I talked to her about one little devil, and, lo! here is another. That makes two who possess me, if King Jamie's right. I'll just have a little of the devilish weed before I go out. Nay, resist the devil, and he will flee from thee. Go, little devil, back to thy place, and let's see what our good Protestant King does say."

He put back the pipe, and took from his scantily-furnished shelves a copy of his Majesty's Counterblast against Tobacco, seated himself comfortably, and began to read.

Master Peasegood's countenance was a study : for what he read did not seem to agree with him. He frowned, he pursed up his lips, he nodded, he shook his head ; and at last, after half-an-hour's study, he dashed the book down upon the floor, doubled his fist, and brought it heavily upon the table.

" If this book had not been written by our sovereign lord, James the First, by the Grace of God King of Great Britain, France, and Ireland, as it says in the dedication to my Bible—and what a thumping lie it is—I should say that it was the work of one of the silliest, most dunder-headed, and bumble-brained fools who ever walked God's earth. Tchah, tchah, tchah, tchah. I don't believe the pipe's a little devil after all.

"Here! I must be off," he said, with a sigh. "There's work to be done. I'll go see my poor old friend Cobbe, and try and comfort him in his trouble.

"Nay, I will not; it will be like running right into temptation. He'll bring out pipes and ale.

"But he is in trouble sore, and I have not been of late. I must go—

"'Into temptation.'

"Nay, it cannot be into temptation, for it is to do good works. The ale is not a devil of possession, after all.

"Mistress Hilberry, I'm going down to Jeremiah Cobbe, if any one should call."

"All right, master," she said; and the stout parson rolled out, and sauntered down to the cottage the founder occupied now.

"Ah! Master Cobbe," he cried, "I've been remiss in visiting you these last few weeks, but I'm glad to see thee look so well."

"Well? Master Peasegood," said the founder, sadly. "Nay, I am not well. Perhaps I am, though—perhaps I am. I have been busy lately, very busy. A goodly store of cannon and ammunition has been sent off to his Majesty this past week."

"Ay, so I hear," said the parson.

"But sit down, man. Hey, Mrs. Croftly, bring a flagon of ale and the pipes and to-bacco. Master Peasegood will sit down here in the garden with me this evening."

"That I will," was the hearty response.

A table was placed on one side, and the two friends sat down, drank heartily to one another, and then filled, lit their pipes, and smoked in silence for awhile."

"There's a nice view from here, Master Cobbe," said the parson at last.

" Ay, there is," said the founder; and a longing painful look came upon his deeply-lined face, as he thrust back his rough, white hair and sighed.

" A very pretty view. You like this spot ? "

" Yes," said the founder, slowly, as he pointed with the stem of his little pipe to an opening in the forest beyond the ruins of the Pool-house. " Do you see yon patch of rock where the martins have made their nests ?"

" Surely, surely," said Master Peasegood.

" There is a good-sized hole there, friend Peasegood."·

" Yes, I see," said Master Peasegood, nodding, " though my eyes are not what they were."

" That place was made by the shell fired from my big howitzer when my poor girl applied the match."

" Poor child ! " said Master Peasegood,

sadly, and for some time the two men sat and smoked in silence.

"Shall you ever build up the house again, Master Cobbe?" said the parson at last.

The founder turned upon him almost fiercely, and seemed about to utter some angry word; but he calmed down, took the parson's fat hand in his, shook it, and released it.

"Nay," he said, "let it rest; let it rest."

"I did not want to hurt your feelings, Master Cobbe," said the parson; "but I thought it would be better for it and for thee. You must be growing richer than before."

"Yes; and what good is it?" said the founder, bitterly. "Of what use is money to me? I only work and toil to keep my mind at rest. Nay, nay, I cannot build the old place up; let it be. Besides," he added dryly, "Mother Goodhugh says it is cursed."

"Hang Mother Goodhugh—or burn her," cried the parson impetuously. "A wicked, cursing, old hag. She had better mend her ways, or Sir Thomas will be laying her by the heels. He swore he would months ago, but I persuaded him not. She had been following and abusing Mistress Anne."

"Ay, poor soul—poor soul, she is mad from her grief, and it makes her curse. Ah! parson, many's the time I could have gone about cursing too. Poor soul—poor soul! let her rest."

"I see you have been very busy with the garden again."

"Ay; it is getting to be what it was. The trees have shot forth once more, and the flowers bloom. She loved that garden, parson—dearly."

"Ay; and the old house too, Master Cobbe. Build it up, man; build it up."

"Nay, not a stone. It is cursed—cursed."

"Bah! Stuff, man. Away with such folly. It is no more cursed than it is haunted, as the people say."

The founder started, and gazed strangely at his friend.

"Do they say it is haunted?"

"Yes; such folly. Two or three people have sworn to me that they have heard shrieks."

"Parson," said the founder hoarsely, as he laid his hand on the other's sleeve; "they are right; I once heard them too."

"What?" said Master Peasegood, laughing, "the owls?"

"Nay, I should know the cry of an owl, man. It is not that. Time after time I've stood there in the forest, and heard the wild cry just at dark when everything is still."

"Nay, nay," said Master Peasegood, "the dead don't cry for help, neither do the angels in heaven; and if there's truth in all we believe, man, our little Mace's looking down upon us, an angel among God's best and dearest ones."

The old man's head went down upon his

hand at this, and he sat in silence for some time, while, with his eyes misty and dim, Master Peasegood leaned back in his chair, and smoked with all his might.

The silence was broken by the founder holding out his hand to his visitor, and shaking it warmly.

"Thankye, parson, thankye," he said. "What you say ought to be true; and I hope she forgives me for my vanity and pride."

"Poor child! It was a mistake, Master Cobbe, but let it rest. They say our gay spark, Sir Mark, is going to comfort himself by wedding Mistress Anne."

"Ay? Indeed?" said the founder. "I did hear something of the kind, but I paid little heed."

"I hear it as a fact, Master Cobbe."

"Well, let him," said the founder. "He should be a rich man, too, by this time, for he has made money from me as well as I have from the King. Don't talk of it, though; it makes me dwell upon the past."

They smoked on for a time without speaking, and then, with a patient, piteous aspect in his face, the founder turned to his visitor.

"I've been a wicked man, parson," he said.

"So we all are," said Master Peasegood, bluffly. "I always sinned from a desire for the good things of this life. I love goodly food, and good ale, and good tobacco now; and I shall go on sinning to the end," he added, taking a hearty draught.

"I have been harsh and hard, and I've not done my duty here, Master Peasegood; and these punishments have come upon me for my sins."

"Stuff, stuff!" cried Master Peasegood. "I won't sit and hear it. Don't talk of your Maker as if he were some petty, revengeful man like us, ready to visit every little weakness upon our heads with a misfortune, or to pay us for being good boys with a slice of bread and honey. Out on such religious ideas as that, Master Cobbe, and think of your God as one who is great and good. Bah! It aggravates me to hear and see people fall down and worship the ugly image they have set up in their hearts, one that every work of the Creator gives the lie to for its falsity and cruel wrong. Bear your burden, Jeremiah Cobbe, like a man. It is not in us to know the ins and outs of God's ways; and it is a wicked and impious sin for people to say this is a judgment, or that is a judgment, and to pretend to know what the All-Seeing thinks and does. You say you've been a wicked man, Master Cobbe."

"Yes, yes," said the founder sadly; "and I have but one hope now, and that is that I may see my darling once again."

"Amen to that," said Master Peasegood; "but, as to your wickedness, I wish every man was as wicked, and hot-tempered, and true-hearted, and generous, and frank, and industrious, and forgiving as thou art, Jeremiah Cobbe; and —— Will you have that ale flagon filled again ? Much talking makes me dry."

The founder smiled, and called for Croftly's wife, who replenished the flagon, bobbed a curtsey to the parson, and re-entered the cottage.

" I like you, Jeremiah Cobbe," continued Master Peasegood, after setting down the flagon with a satisfied sigh; " but don't be superstitious, man, like our sovereign master the King, who has written a book to hand down his wisdom to posterity."

" Indeed!" said the founder, whose thoughts were evidently far away.

" Yes, indeed," said Master Peasegood; " and it's all about witches and warlocks and the like. That piece of idiot spawn has gotten itself down here into Sir Thomas's hands; and, as I told thee, he was very near

laying that foolish old woman Mother Goodhugh by the heels. Now she hates me like
poison, because I laugh at her and tell the
people she is a half-crazed old crone. Last
time I saw her we quarrelled, for I told her
she was a wretched old impostor, for cheat-
ing the poor people as she did. Ha! ha!
ha! and then she defied and cursed me, and
said she'd go to Father Brisdone and turn
Roman Catholic. I told her to go, and he'd
curse her for cursing, for it is his trade,
and she has no right to handle such tools
at all."

"Poor weak woman," said the founder.
"She is more to be pitied than blamed. I
suppose she thinks in her heart that I am the
cause of all her woes."

"Ay, poor soul, but it's partly vanity,
friend Cobbe. She likes to set up for a
prophetess, a sort of diluted Deborah, and to
make the people believe in her. There, you
must go and see her. If I go to her, being

the good man of the parish, she will have naught to say to me. Now, you being a wicked man, may have more influence than I."

" I influence ? Nay, man ; she'll fall a cursing if I go nigh her cot."

" Let her curse. Her words won't hurt thee, man. Go to her, and give her money —thou hast enough—bid her get away far enough from this place to somewhere safe ; and when there, tell her to live a decent life and forget her silly trickstering and stuff. It's a fine opportunity for thee, Jeremiah Cobbe. It's just the sort of revenge thou lik'st to take on an enemy. Go and pour coals of fire on her head, for I'm sure this place isn't safe for such as she."

" Would Sir Thomas imprison her ?" said the founder.

" Sir Thomas is so good and honest a justice of the peace, and so great a lover of the words of his Majesty the King, who made him the baronet he is, that he would set up a stake, scatter Dame Beckley's dried simples and herbs around it, heap it with goodly faggots, and burn Mother Good-hugh for a witch while the Roehurst people would look on."

"Thinkest thou this, Master Peasegood?"

"I'm sure of it," said the parson, dashing down his pipe in his anger. "Jeremiah Cobbe, it makes me as mad as Moses to see what fools the people are. We have just got rid of the superstitions of Rome, sir, and we go at once and set up the golden calf of witchcraft, and worship it, from our ruler to the humblest peasant in his realm. By my word, Master Cobbe, an' I had had the two tables in my hands like the old prophet, I'd not have broken them on the rocks, but upon the thick-boned skulls of my erring folk."

"Not worship the idol—condemn it, Master Peasegood," said the founder, smiling

" Well, but we believe it," cried the other. " Out upon us all, but we are sorry fools."

" I'll go and do this thing, Master Peasegood," said the founder, after musing for a few minutes.

" That's right; I knew thou would'st."

" But maybe she will not go."

" Then take her, like the angels did Lot of old, and thrust her out of the place. Tell her Roehurst will prove a Sodom to her if she does not go, for i' faith she'll go to the flames, in spite of all I can do or say."

" I'll go to her this very evening, Master Peasegood."

" Then I will go my way," cried the parson; and, paying one more attention to the flagon, he rose, shook hands, and left.

<hr>

CHAPTER X.

HOW MOTHER GOODHUGH FARED ILL AT JUSTICE'S HANDS.

By chance it happened that Anne Beckley had extended her walk towards the woods and had strolled farther than she had intended. Fate led her into the narrow lane where she had rested in Gil Carr's arms when Mace and Sir Mark had been witnesses of the scene.

She smiled now as she seated herself upon the bank, and thought of the changes that had taken place, for she was shortly to become Mark Leslie's wife.

How the time had passed, she thought, and how cleverly she had won Sir Mark from his gloom and despondency to become at first grateful, then loving, and at last—so she believed—so infatuated with her, that she could do with him as she pleased.

If some unkind friend had told her that her father's money and estates had anything to do with the match, she would have rejected the suggestion with scorn, and then gone to her mirror, to examine the sit of her ruffle, to give a slight touch to her painted cheeks, and perhaps add another ornamental patch to her chin.

Sir Mark was in town now, preparing for the bridal, and Anne's heart was joyful within her, as she thought of the coming ceremony. For years she had been dreaming of and hoping for wedlock, and at last she was to be a wife—a lady of title—Dame Anne Leslie, and her eyes sparkled with the pleasure of the thought.

The spot she had chosen for her reverie, though, brought up thoughts that made her sigh. There, close by where she was seated, Gil Carr had held her in his arms; and she sighed as she recalled how fondly she believed that she had loved him. And where was he now?

A year had rolled by since he set sail, and no news of either him or his followers had reached Roehurst since; and as she thought of this the events of that terrible time came crowding back.

" Poor Mace ! " she said, softly; " I am sorry I hated you so much; and poor Gil Carr, he was a proper youth. Alack! What change one lives to see ! "

She felt half disposed to continue her walk, and go on as far as the Pool-house; but a slight shudder ran through her nerves at the thought. Somehow the ruins had a repelling influence upon her, and she shrank from going near, feeling that she had been to blame for what had taken place on that terrible night.

"I don't think I'll go," she said softly; and she was about to rise and return, when she became aware that some one was standing close behind her, and, starting up, she found herself face to face with Mother Goodhugh, who had advanced as quietly as a cat.

"Mother Goodhugh!" she cried in a startled voice.

"Yes, my dearie, it be Mother Goodhugh. What can I do for thee, my beauty bird?"

"Nothing, mother," replied Anne sharply.

"Nothing, my dearie?" said the old woman laughing. "Nay, surely you want some help of the poor old woman who works to help you. Is it a new lover, my dear?"

"I have told thee I do not want anything, mother," cried Anne peevishly.

"Nay, then, come on to my cottage, where we can talk. Thou has not been to see me for months and months."

"Nay, mother, I'll come no more. Good day, I must get me home."

"Stay, child," cried Mother Goodhugh, clutching at her dress; "I want to talk to thee of him. Come to my place."

"Loose me this instant, mother," cried Mistress Anne, indignantly. "How darest thou lay thy hands on me?"

"Only because we are sisters, dearie."

"Sisters?"

"Ay, dearie; don't we practise the art together. But hist, hist, come to my cottage and let us talk."

"Not a step will I go," cried Anne, angrily.

"Nay, is it so? Ah, she has gotten what she wanted by my help—a brave, fine husband, and now she throws me by."

"Cease thy talk about those childish follies. I am sick of them."

"Ay, child, yes; thou art sick of them now, but when thou wast hungry for thy love nothing was too good for Mother Goodhugh then."

" Out upon thee ! Did I not pay thee well
for thy silly mummeries ? "

" Pay me well ? " cried Mother Goodhugh. " Nay; what were a few paltry gold
pieces for such a husband as I gained for
thee ? "

" You gained for me ? " cried Anne,
contemptuously.

" Ay, to be sure, I gained for thee, mistress; and now thou hast him safe I be
thrown aside. Not once hast thou been to
me these many months."

" I tell thee I have done with such follies,"
cried Anne contemptuously. " I have paid
thee, and there the matter ends."

" Oh, nay, mistress, it does not. Thou
hast thy lover, and so had poor Mace Cobbe,
and the wedding was to be next day; but I
prophesied that she should not have the man
of thy choice, and what came to pass ? "

" Mother Goodhugh," said Anne, turning

pale, "if I thought thou had'st anything to do with that misfortune at the Pool thou should'st be handed over to my father for punishment according to thy deserts."

"And would she who helped me be punished too?"

"If thou had'st accomplices, yes."

"Sweet mistress, then we will go to prison, thou and I, together, for we made our plans to stay the wedding of Mace Cobbe."

"It is false; I had nothing to do with thy plans," cried Anne excitedly.

"Had'st thou not better come to my cottage, mistress?" said Mother Goodhugh.

"Nay, I have done with thee and thy ways. I'll come there no more."

"But thou wilt pay me for winning thee a husband."

"Pay thee?" cried Anne contemptuously. "What should I pay thee?"

" A hundred golden pounds, mistress," cried the old woman, whose eyes sparkled at the very mention of so much money.

" A hundred pence," cried Anne. " Go, get you gone, old crone. I'll never part with a piece again for thy follies."

" Have a care, mistress," cried the old woman excitedly, for her anger was getting the better of her reason. " Thou art not Mark Leslie's wife as yet, and some accident might happen to thee, too."

" Mother Goodhugh," cried Anne, " have a care. Thou art a marked woman."

" I will have a care, my dearie, that if I am to suffer, thou shalt suffer too. I can place thee in prison if I am touched, so beware—beware."

" Vile old hag," cried Anne angrily; " Speak a word against me, and you shall bitterly repent it."

" Rue it, eh! We'll see; we'll see," cried the old woman, shaking her stick after the girl, as she hurried back, uneasy enough in her mind to suffer acutely, for Mother Goodhugh might throw obstacles in the way. She shuddered at the bare thought of what had happened on the eve of Mace's wedding, but determined to risk all.

"If she speaks, no one will believe her," cried Anne laughing. " She shall be seized for a witch, and she dare not charge me with helping her, for if she did it would only be accusing herself, and that she dare not do. Neither dare I let her be at liberty till I am dear Mark's wife. After this she may do her worst."

Full of this intent—for now that the old woman had obtruded herself once more upon her path, she really feared her—Anne hurried back towards the Moat, feeling anything but secure while Mother Goodhugh was at liberty. Her mind had been too much occupied of late during Sir Mark's long visits to trouble herself about the old woman, and whatever thought she had had of the terrible night at the Pool-house had been gradually allowed to grow dull. The great thing had been that the wedding had been stayed, but, now that she thought the matter over, she felt sure that Mother Goodhugh had been guilty of some desperate deed; and to bring it home to herself—if the old woman would do such a thing for gain, might she not do it for revenge?

Anne shuddered and her brow grew cloudy as she felt that she could not set Mother Goodhugh aside as one that she need not fear. Sir Mark was not yet her husband, and what if some terrible catastrophe were to happen to prevent the wedding.

"I should go mad," she muttered; and she paused to think whether it would be better to try a bribe.

" She wants too much money, and if I did silence her now she would be pestering me with claims for more, and threaten and harass me. No, mother; you have opened the battle again, so now let us see which of us is the stronger."

Hurrying to her father's room lest her mind should change, Anne had a long colloquy with him, introducing the subject of witchcraft incidentally.

"Sir Mark tells me, father, that his Majesty strongly approves of efforts being made to keep down witches in this country."

"Yes, my dear, so I heard Sir Mark say," replied Sir Thomas, putting on his carp-like visage, and gaping and panting at his daughter, as his eyes stood out wide and round.

"Why should you not do something to commend yourself to the King?"

"But what could I do, child?" said Sir Thomas.

"True, there is nothing you could, unless you arrested Mother Goodhugh."

"You forbad it once, but the very thing!" cried Sir Thomas, eagerly.

"But she is not a witch," said Anne, dubiously.

"Nay, my child, but, according to his Majesty's book, she has all the signs of a witch in her."

"Indeed, father?"

"Yes, child, I have studied it all well, and can show you a dozen points wherein she answers to a witch. Anne, my child, she shall be seized and examined."

"I don't think I would, father. Such women are sure to say more than is quite true, and spit their venom at random. Better let her rest in peace."

"Nay, child, she shall be examined, and, if she says too much, she shall be gagged. I am not a man to be trifled with by a known and practised witch."

Next day Mother Goodhugh returned to her cottage from one of her many absences in the forest, full of bitterness against Mistress Anne.

"Does she think she be going to play with me?" muttered the old woman. "Not she. I be not frightened of her threats now. Let her speak if she dares. I could tell strange tales against her if I liked, and I'll be paid. One hundred golden pounds she shall give me, or she shall not marry him; nay, that she shall not. Mother Goodhugh is stronger than they think." She chuckled, as she walked sharply up and down the little room, shaking her stick and then thumping the end upon the floor. "Nice tales could I tell. Mistress Anne Beckley would look well as my companion, and ha-ha-ha! ho-ho-ho! What would the fine, gay, gallant Sir Mark say to his sweet if he knew of the tricks and plans she had carried out. There would be an end to the wedding, and she dare not speak. What do you want here?"

"I came to see thee, Mother Goodhugh," said the founder, who had just raised the latch, and stood in the doorway.

"To see me," cried the old woman, fiercely. "What! hast come to be cursed again? But no, no, no; go away, man, go away, away," she said hurriedly, as she fell a trembling. "I don't want thee here."

"Mother Goodhugh," said the founder, sadly, "thou hast always looked upon me as an enemy."

"Yes, a bitter, cruel enemy," she cried, flinching from him. Then, with a malignant grin, she added, "But thou hast had to suffer too, Master Cobbe, and to know what it is to gnaw thy heart with pain."

"Yes, yes, woman, I know all that," said the founder, hastily; "but let us not talk of the by-gone, but of the future."

"What is my future to thee, Mas' Jeremiah Cobbe?" cried the old woman, suspiciously. "Go thy ways, and let me go mine."

"I came to tell thee that there is danger for thee, Mother Goodhugh. They say that thou'rt a witch, and I came to bid thee go hence to some place where thou art not known."

"Who will harm me?" cried the old woman.

"Maybe Sir Thomas will have thee put in prison."

"She daren't do it—she daren't do it," cried the old woman, fiercely. "I defy her —I defy her."

"The law dare do a good deal, Mother Goodhugh," said the founder, sadly. "But take my advice: go from hence. I have ready for thee twenty gold pounds; they will keep thee for some time, and when they are gone I will give thee more. But go, and go at once, before it is too late."

The old woman's fingers were held out crooked and trembling to grasp the money, her eyes twinkling with eagerness; but ere the founder could place the coins therein she seemed to make a tremendous effort over herself, and snatched back her hands.

"Nay," she cried, "I will not go. Thou for one would'st get rid of me, and Mistress Anne hath sent thee, but I'll not be baulked of my revenge."

"I came not from Mistress Anne, good mother. It was from a talk with Master Peasegood that I came to-day."

"Yes, yes, I know," cried the old woman, exultingly, "from Mas' Peasegood, her friend. So I am to be sent away on a beggar's pittance, and forego my revenge. She be a clever girl, but she can't outwit me."

"I understand not thy sayings, mother," said the founder, wearily ; "I only bid thee get hence, for the sake of thy poor dead husband and thy boy."

The founder said the words in all kind-
ness, but they transformed Mother Goodhugh into a perfect fury; her eyes flashed,
the foam stood upon her lips, and, mouthing
and gibbering in impotent rage, she pointed
to the door.

"Go," she shrieked at last, "and tell
them who sent thee that Mother Goodhugh
will stay in her place and defy them. Bid
Mistress Anne have a care, and tell her that
if Mother Goodhugh stands at the stake it
will be back to back with the mincing,
painting, and patching madam who came
and bade her curse and destroy her rival at
the Pool-house; who planned its destruction; who is a worse witch than I. Tell
her all this, for I'll stay and defy her. Bid
her do her worst."

"Silence, woman!" cried the founder, who
gazed at her, horrified and startled at this
outburst; "thou art mad."

"Mad? Ay, mad, if thou wilt; but wait

and see. Tell her I'll stay—tell her I'll stay and defy her. She don't know Mother Goodhugh yet, Jeremiah Cobbe; so wait and see."

"I shall not have long to wait, then," said the founder, gloomily. "It is thy own fault, woman, and God forgive thee for thy cursing and thy lies."

Mother Goodhugh had literally driven him from her room, to stand at the doorway fiercely gesticulating and threateningly waving her stick; but, as the founder spoke and drew back from her, a complete change came over the old woman: her eyes grew fixed, her jaw dropped, the stick fell from her hand, and she clung to the doorpost, turning of a deadly white, for at that moment Sir Thomas Beckley, looking red, important, and accompanied by the village constable, a couple of assistants with a cart, and some dozen or two of the people, came slowly to the door.

The rustic constable held a document in his hand, which he tried to read to the woman, and dismally failed from want of erudition, even though prompted by Sir Thomas. He mumbled out, though, something about the heinous sin of witchcraft; and sovereign lord and King.

Then thrusting the document into his rough doublet, he caught the old woman by the wrist.

"No, no," she shrieked in agony, all her defiance gone, as she found herself face to face with the horrible reality. "No, no, I will not go."

"Come, thou must, Mother Goodhugh," said the constable; "and I warn thee that if thou begin'st any cursing against me and my men it will be the worse for thee."

"I will not go; I am innocent, Sir Thomas. Pray, Sir Thomas, don't let him. A poor weak widow woman. Pray, pray don't."

"An anointed witch thou art," said the justice, pompously. "Away with her."

"Nay, nay, Sir Thomas," cried the founder. "She is no witch; only a silly, half-mad creature."

"Yes, that be right," cried Mother Goodhugh, clinging frantically to one of the doorposts, "mad—mad with trouble, good Sir Thomas."

"Nay, woman, thy witchcrafts have stunk in my nostrils this many a day, and there is a long list of crimes for thee to expiate at the stake."

"Shame, Sir Thomas!" cried the founder, indignantly; "if any one has cause against her it is I."

"Yes, yes, good Sir Thomas, hear him. I have cursed him more than any. Oh, pray, pray."

"Pray," cried the justice; "pray to thy familiars, woman! Take her along."

"This is monstrous," cried the founder, indignantly.

"Hold thy peace, Master Cobbe," said Sir Thomas, impatiently; "and if thou dost interfere it will be at thy peril. Take her away, men, take her away."

"No, no! no, no!" shrieked the horrified woman, before whose affrighted face the faggot and stake already loomed. "Mas' Cobbe, save me—for pity's sake, save me. I be not a witch. I only cursed in the naughtiness of my heart. Help me, Mas' Cobbe; for thy dear child's sake, help me, and I'll tell thee all. I will not go. I will not go."

The founder sprang forward to her help, but he was unarmed, and Sir Thomas drew his sword and placed himself before the prisoner.

"I warn thee, Master Cobbe," he cried, "that this is a legal seizure. Stand back, sir, stand back. Quick, men, do your duty."

It was a horrible scene, for the old woman clung to her door, and had to be literally torn away by the men, who, adding coarseness to the superstition of their superiors, felt no mercy for one whom they looked upon as being leagued with the powers of ill.

And now that the wise woman's reign was over, and she was held to be harmless, those who had feared and sought counsel of her rose up to spit on the shivering form that was being dragged along the ground towards the tail of the cart. For we were a fine and manly race in the good old times, and those who represented us at Roehurst made no scruple about reviling and kicking the quivering, helpless creature, who struggled hard as she was dragged by the wrists, her clothes torn, her hair dishevelled, and her old white face looking from one to the other for the help that none would give.

"Out upon the witch!" they shrieked and yelled, drowning the poor wretch's hoarse cries for mercy. "Burn her! Burn her!" rose in chorus; and the founder strove hard to reach her, but he was kept back by the increasing crowd, for the news that Mother Goodhugh was to be taken for a witch soon spread, and men, women, and children came panting up to join in execrating the helpless wretch.

Faint and exhausted, they bound her hands behind her back and her ankles tightly together, before, amidst tremendous shouting and yelling, she was lifted by four strong men, and literally thrown into, the cart, which was then set in motion, with Sir Thomas following behind with his sword drawn, and the people going before and crowding after, as the wheels sank down first on one side in the ruts, then on the other, revealing the wretched woman, who was now goaded to desperation, and had struggled up into a kneeling position, which she could hardly maintain for the rolling of the cart.

Every time she was nearly thrown down the crowd yelled with delight; and, on some rustic genius throwing a clod of earth at her, his example was followed, and the poor wretch knelt there cowering from the shower of missiles sent into the cart.

At last she contrived to get her wrists loosed from the ill-tied cords; and, holding the cart-side with one hand, she raised the other, and shrieked out anathema after anathema against her persecutors, uttering such horrible curses against them that the less bold shrank away and the stoutest began to quail. But Mother Goodhugh's reign of cursing was nearly at an end; for, as the founder indignantly watched the proceedings, a great lad close by him picked up and hurled a lump of sandrock at the wretched creature, striking her full in the temple, and, amidst a shout of triumph, the miserable woman fell stunned and bleeding to the bottom of the cart.

" That were a good hurl, master," cried the lout, with a broad grin.

" Yes," said the founder, fiercely, " and so was that ! "

As he spoke, he struck the great, broad-faced fellow straight in the cheek, and he rolled over into one of the cart-ruts, whilst the procession with Mother Goodhugh, fortunately insensible now to pain, turned a corner of the winding lane, and passed out of the founder's sight.

CHAPTER XI.

HOW ROEHURST KEPT FETE FOR A WEDDING AND A DEATH.

TRULY Satan must have been reigning upon earth in full fig when it was found necessary to execute thirty of his disciples at one time in Edinburgh. As for poor Mrs. Hicks and her little daughter, aged nine, who were hanged at Huntingdon in 1716, they might have rejoiced at the opportunity of getting out of such a world of fools and ignorance. They must have been great sinners, though, for they had sold their souls to the devil, and —crowning atrocity!—they had raised a storm, and the recipe is handed down to posterity, for the *modus operandi* was " pulling off their stockings and making a lather of soap!"

If for such a crime as this a tender child of nine could be punished with death in Christian England in those salutary days, there can be no wonder that Mother Goodhugh's condemnation was pretty sure. She was the known witch of the neighbourhood, and those who had feared her, sought her help, and paid her, were among the first to give evidence against the repository of their secrets.

Jeremiah Cobbe strove hard to save her, and so did Master Peasegood; but two men in an out-of-the-way part of England could not stem the tide of popular opinion, as it set strong against the wretched woman. In her rage and hate she strove to drag down Mistress Anne as well, but in so doing made a bitter enemy of one who was strong in court favour. For on hearing of the accusation Sir Mark lost no opportunity of fighting against " this notorious witch."

But Mother Goodhugh was not condemned without ample test and trial, fallen as she had under the care of a famous witch-finder and judge of the day, who came down to the nearest town by royal command to investigate the case.

The wretched woman was put through a course of torture. She suffered the pin test for the witch's mark. This failing, she next had her thumbs and toes tied together, she was wrapped in a sheet, and in the presence of plenty of spectators thrown into a pool.

As a certain amount of air remained in the sheet, and the water was some time in penetrating it, the poor woman naturally enough floated, amidst the execrations of the crowd, among whom were some twenty or thirty of Sir Mark's men.

None but a witch could float, so it was said; so after a final test, in which Mother

Goodhugh failed to repeat the Lord's prayer without hesitation, her trial proceeded, and she was condemned to be burnt at the stake in her own village a week after sentence.

There was not much mercy shown in those days, and, though the fair rounded cheeks of Anne Beckley turned a little pale when Sir Mark brought her the news, they flushed directly after, for she felt that she would be freed from a persecutor who would give her no rest, and who might cause her trouble with her husband after the first few months of matrimonial life.

Besides, Anne Beckley argued with a shudder, the old woman had done strange things, and, with the superstition in her nature ready to accept it, she argued that if living she might curse her to her injury. True she might curse her now, but, as her accusations had been set aside as malicious, it was quite possible that her evil genius had deserted her as he did those who became unfortunate, and, as she had risked so much and gained only defiance, Anne Beckley determined to go on to the end.

It was a strange mixture, but the preparations for the wedding of Mistress Anne Beckley and for the execution of Mother Goodhugh went on side by side, in spite of the further efforts of Master Peasegood and the founder, who even went so far as to make a journey to London to seek the King's clemency. Of course without avail.

From his position as maker of his Majesty's Ordnance, Master Cobbe succeeded in getting an audience, to be received well, told that he was a good man, that his guns were strong, but that he knew naught of witchcraft.

" Read my book, Master Cobbe, read my book," said his Majesty; and Jeremiah Cobbe had to bow himself out with the stout parson, who was perspiring with anger.

" I'm a loyal and I hope religious man,

Master Cobbe," said the latter excitedly; "I fear God and I honour the King; but all the same, Master Cobbe, I vow and declare that his Majesty is the damnedest fool I ever saw, and may the Lord forgive me for swearing."

"Yes," said the founder, sadly. "Well, old friend, we have done all we can, so let us stay away till they have wreaked their silly vengeance on that poor, mad soul."

"No, no, thank God!" said Master Pease-good, "they can only wreak it on her body, my friend, and as to staying here—nay, that must not be. I have no love for the weak old creature, who spent her time in mummery and silly cursing, but my place is by her side to ask forgiveness with her and a pain-less passage to the mercy-seat."

"Ay, parson, thou art right, and I'll join thee in thy prayer, for there should be mercy for one who men declare shall have her hellish flames before she dies."

"I don't quite like that speech, Master Cobbe, but you mean quite right. Now, good friend, take me to some hostel and give me ale, or I shall faint here by the way. Nay, I'll not. It is choler. I'll be blooded instead, a good nine ounces, or I shall have a fit."

They were stout, strong posts that were set up outside the Moat gates to bear the arch of evergreens and flowers, but it was a stronger one in front of the cottage where Mother Goodhugh had spent her days, and, while men piled last year's faggots and heaped up charcoal taken from the founder's dogwood stacks, others cut down branches of yew and holly and gathered bundles of heather and golden gorse, and the preparations for the wedding feast went on.

"Ah, parson," cried Sir Mark, from the back of one of Sir Thomas's stout cobs, as he rode along beside fair Mistress Anne, who was mounted on a handsome jennet, " I have not seen thee for days. Art ready to tie our nuptial knot?"

" No, Sir Mark," said Master Peasegood, sternly. "I am going to pray beside the dying and the dead."

" What does he mean—the insolent fool?" cried Sir Mark, angrily.

" Truth, love, I cannot tell," said Mistress Anne; but in her heart of hearts she felt a sickening sensation, and would have given anything that the execution or the coming wedding were to take place elsewhere.

" As he will, sweetest," said Sir Mark, tenderly, and they rode on, receiving salutations from all they passed; "there are plenty of priests who will be glad to make us one; and only think, love—only two days now."

Anne Beckley rode on in silence for some time, thinking. Her betrothed laughed and chatted gaily, and truly they were a handsome pair; but the girl's heart was ill at ease, and at last, being bantered by Sir Mark upon her silence, she leaned towards him in a quiet glade of the forest, and, laying her hand upon his shoulder, offered her lips to his long clinging kiss.

"I have a favour to ask, love," she said.

"Ask favours from now till night, and thou shalt have them all," he cried.

"It is but one," faltered Anne; "our wedding."

"I would it were over," cried Sir Mark, eagerly; "but what of it, bright eyes?"

"I like not the day," said Anne, checking her horse's pace so that she could cling to her companion.

"And why not?" he asked.

"I like it not for my sake and thine," she said in a low tone.

"Let's hear the reason on thy part," said Sir Mark, laughing.

"It is the day they burn that wicked

woman; and it troubles me that we should go to church at such a time."

" The day of a good deed, love," he said. " Now the other, for my sake."

" Have you not thought," she said, pressing closer to him, heedless of the fact that they were watched.

" I thought? Yes, that it is the most blessed day in the calendar."

" Nay; but have you not thought what day it is?"

" Not I.   Saint Somebody-or-another's— some Christian martyr's, perhaps; and we'll give him a burnt sacrifice of bad witch to satisfy his manes."

" Mark, it is the anniversary of the day that was to have seen you a husband; me a broken-hearted girl."

Sir Mark started and changed colour. He was troubled, for it seemed a bad augury that such a day should have been chosen, but he lightly put it aside.

" Never mind, love ; it was an accident, and can make no difference now. Besides, the matter is settled, and if we picked the days over we should find each the anniversary of some troubled time."

Anne Beckley was disappointed, but she made no more objection, and they rode soon after through the avenue and over the bridge, beneath which the great carp gaped and stared with their big round eyes in unconscious imitation of their master, the wise dispenser of King James's justice, and keeper of the peace.

CHAPTER XII.

EARLY morning, as bright and glowing autumn time as ever shone over the weald of Sussex. The harvest was gathered in; the trees were heavy beneath the red and golden crop of apples, and in hedgerow and plantation the brown and cream-husked nuts peered out in clusters from the leafy stubs.

There was a suspicion here and there of the coming fall, but only in bright touches of beauty—golds, and russets, and reds—bloody crimson, and orange scarlet, where the sun-kissed leaves yet burned beneath the caresses of the ardent god. The sky above was of the richest, purest blue, and the eye rested on naught but beauty, so long as it kept to nature, and not to art, for winding along the narrow lane towards Roehurst was a procession of armed men, preceding and following a rough country tumbril, drawn by a clumsy horse. The load was apparently a heap of shabby garments, dropped in one corner of the cart.

But the crowd that pressed upon the armed men, striving to get a glimpse of the interior of the vehicle, could see that the bundle of clothes in the cart moved slightly from time to time, lifting a thin white hand and letting it fall heavily once more ; and as they buzzed, and talked, and shouted to one another, they made out further that there was a grey head raised from the heap, and a white, scared face looked round partly in wonder, partly seeking for pity, as its owner seemed to realise her position, and then crouched lower and lower as she heard shouts and voices crying out the words,

" Mother Goodhugh! Witch! The stake, the stake!"

The escort took the pressure of the eager little crowd very good-humouredly, but had to keep waving the sight-seers back, or some would have been trampled beneath the horse's feet, and as it was the procession was greatly delayed.

" I don't believe they'll burn her after all," said one rough specimen of a peasant to another.

" Nay, they will. Stake be all ready, and faggots enough to burn a dozen such witches as old Mother there."

" I'll believe it when I see it, lad. See if she don't go off in a flash, or else make the rain come so as the faggots won't burn. Nay, lad, she won't be done for yet. Look there. Did'st see her wicked old eyes glowering round when she raised her head? Don't let her look at thee, or she'll put a curse in thy face."

" Ay, but she be a wicked looking one, and it will be a glad riddance for Roehurst when she be gone, for she did naught but curse."

" Mas' Cobbe ought to be glad to see her burnt, for she's cursed him oft enough, poor soul."

" But why don't they make haste? I want to see the burning, and then get back to the wedding games."

" Oh, they won't wed till Mother Good-hugh's all in ash, lad. See, there be the bridegroom. He be going to see it done."

" But what be they stopping for?"

" Don't know," said the other, climbing up the bank and holding on by the branch of a tree. " Why, it be parson come, and he be getting into the cart with Mother Good-hugh. Say, look there! He be gone down on his knees aside her, and takes her hand. Look out, parson, as she don't fly at thee like a cat."

But there was no cat-like spring in Mother Goodhugh, for torture and starvation had reduced her so that the little life left in her was likely to flutter away before the torch was placed to the faggots. As Master Pease-good laboriously clambered into the cart and knelt beside her, he took one of the poor wretch's wasted hands in his, and she raised her head to look up at him half-wonderingly, before letting it fall once more, and remaining apparently nerveless and flaccid, waiting for the end.

The procession passed within fifty yards of the Moat gate, where Anne Beckley was waiting—not to cry out in reviling tones against the wretched woman, but to see her pass, hidden awhile amidst the dense evergreens, and trembling lest she should be seen.

Anne Beckley's heart beat fast as the procession came nearer and nearer, and she crouched down trembling as she fancied that

Mother Goodhugh must see her; while the cold dew stood upon her brow as she waited for the curses the old woman would fling upon her head.

But there was no curse hurled at her; there was the trampling of feet, and the buzz of many voices, beating hoofs, and grinding wheels coming nearer and nearer, till all appeared to stay close by, and Anne's heart seemed to stop its pulse as well.

She had come to see her enemy, and would gladly have witnessed the execution, only that she dared not express a wish so to do; and even now, so great was her trepidation, that in place of gazing at the broken, half-dead object in the cart, she shrank down lower and lower till the leaves completely sheltered her head.

What were they stopping for? Were they going to bring Mother Goodhugh there?

No: there had been no stoppage at all; it was only her fancy. They were going slowly

on, and that was Master Peasegood's voice
praying beside the wretched creature so near
her end.

The buzzing and trampling seemed to grow
louder and the grating of the wheels more
defined, till it seemed to Anne as if they
would never pass away; but they grew fainter
at last, and after some ten minutes of agony
she hurried out of the clump of shrubs, and
hastened to her room, too faint and heartsick
to think of dressing for the ceremony to
come.

Sir Mark and his men would be at the
execution she knew, and when he returned it
would be a signal to her that her enemy was
no more, and she told herself that she would
be able to go to the little church with a
lighter heart.

In imagination she followed the procession
to the narrow lane, and up to the front of
Mother Goodhugh's cottage, where the great
stake had been placed. She saw the wretched

woman bound there, the faggots fired, and seemed to hear her shrieks as she waved her hands and wildly cursed those around. Now she strained at the chain, and strove to tear it away as it grew red hot and burned into her thin white flesh, while the flames rose higher and higher, the faggots crackled, and she even fancied that she could hear the shouting of the people.

How the smoke curled up, half suffocating her at times, and making her hang her head as if dead! Then it was swept away, and the flames rose higher, half hiding the hideously contorted face with a ruddy lurid veil. The flames fluttered and danced, and seemed to Anne as if rejoicing at their task of purifying the earth from the presence of a witch. Then the smoke rose higher, till it formed a heavy canopy above the stake, while the flames played wildly on its lower surface.

Again the flames opened to reveal the figure of Mother Goodhugh. She had ceased to curse now, and with blackened, outstretched hands was appealing to her executioners to set her free.

As she did so Anne started forward with a wild cry.

"It is too horrible—too horrible!" she shrieked. "Father, father, save her before it is too late!" and then, overpowered by the imaginary scene she had conjured up, she tottered a step or two, and sank fainting upon the floor.

CHAPTER XIII.

HOW THE WITCH-FAGGOTS WERE FIRED.

THE scene at the execution was different from that which Anne Beckley painted in her mind. The cart, with its helpless burden, went slowly on, bumping up and down through the ruts of the narrow lane, and the armed escort patiently bore the pressure of the increasing crowd. For every hamlet for ten or fifteen miles round had sent its occupants to see the double show, and every bank and hillock had its gazing faces; while, as the procession drew near to the stake, with its terrible adjuncts, the cart had some difficulty in getting through.

The crowd gave way, however, to the

escort, who pushed them back till a circle was made about the stake, in the midst of which stood Sir Thomas, Sir Mark, and the armed men.

As the cart stopped, Master Peasegood descended, wiping his bare wet forehead, and stood gazing with pallid face as four of the men pressed forward and roughly lifted the condemned woman to the earth.

"Be gentle, men, be gentle," he cried, in tones of remonstrance. "It is a woman with whom ye have to deal."

"A witch—a foul witch—thou mean'st," said one of the men; and there was a yell of execration from the crowd.

"Silence!" roared Master Peasegood, furiously. "Are ye brute beasts, or men, women, and children? Ah, Master Cobbe, are you there?" he cried. "Can nothing be done to save this poor creature here?"

"Yes," said the founder, sternly. "I protest against this terrible outrage in our midst, and I call upon you, good people, to help me to stop it."

There was a murmur in the crowd that gathered round; but it was the murmur of a hungry beast fearful of being robbed of its prey, and not a hand was raised to help the speaker.

"Master Cobbe," cried Sir Mark, sternly, "if thou art not mad, hold thy peace, and let the King's commands be done."

"Water, water," gasped the wretched woman, looking appealingly round.

"Nay, Jezebel, thou shalt have fire," said Sir Thomas. "It is more purifying than water for such as thou."

There was a burst of laughter at the coarse jest, but Master Peasegood strode into the cottage, took a rough earthenware vessel, and, parting the crowd, filled the mug from the clear cold spring, and held it to the wretched woman's lips.

She drank with avidity, and then pressed her thin white lips to the hand that held the vessel, while her eyes gave a grateful look at the face.

"Bless you," she said, in a hoarse whisper, and her lips kept moving quickly.

"Quick," cried Sir Mark; "we are wasting time," and four of the men seized and carried the trembling creature to the stake, where a chain was hanging ready to bind her fast.

But as it happened there was the chain but no means of fastening it, and impatiently throwing it aside they bound her with a cart-rope so that she was upright, for her limbs refused their task, and she had to be held as the rope was twisted round.

" Mas' Cobbe, Mas' Cobbe!" cried Mother Goodhugh, in a hoarse wail.

"Nay, go not nigh to her, Master Cobbe," cried Sir Thomas. " She will only curse thee again."

For answer the founder, who could not tear himself from the spot, strode towards the stake.

"I cannot save thee, Mother Goodhugh," he said, hoarsely.

"Nay, but thou did'st try," said the poor creature, piteously. "Try and forgive me, Mas' Cobbe, for I be a wicked wretch. I have cursed thee, and the curse has fallen back on me. Mace, thy child, be ——"

"Stand aside, Master Cobbe," cried Sir Mark, imperiously. "Now, knaves, do your work quickly. Round with the faggots. Pile them higher, man, the brushwood first and the charcoal last. Quick, we are wasting time."

The founder and Master Peasegood were thrust aside, and a part of the crowd pushed forward to help to build up from a stack at hand the brushwood and faggots round the wretched woman, who hung forward with drooping head, apparently insensible now from weakness and dread; and at last all was ready.

A deep silence fell upon all. The morning sun shone more brightly than ever on the gay autumn woodlands, and the eager crowd that, open-mouthed and staring, awaited the fiery trial.

"Will she screech?" whispered one matron, who had brought a child in arms to see the show, and who kept handing her little one clusters of the great blackberries that grew so plentifully upon the banks, "because if she do I shouldn't like to stay and hear her cry aloud."

"Nay," said another, "she'll not squeal much; she'll take something to keep away the pains."

"Think she will?

"Ay, that she will. She be an anointed witch. See how she lives. You never go to her place but there be meal in plenty, and sugar and bacon too. Where do it come from, eh?"

"Nay, I d'now."

"She makes it all with spells, and calls up plenty for what she wants. Eh, but she be a clever one. I've met her o' nights in the forest, going crouching along; and one night John Piper see her with a white sperrit, going along together hand in hand."

"Eh, did he? What did he say?"

"He never said a word; he dare not; but went down flat upon his face, and laid there till she'd gone."

"I'd ha' spoke to her if it had been me."

"Nay, thou wouldn't. It be too dreadful. Maybe she'd ha' put a spell upon thee, and cursed thee like, and then thou'd ha' pined away like Susan Harron. You marn't speak to a witch when she be out o' nights."

"But dost think she do conjure up meal, and sugar, and bacon?"

“ Why, could she get ’em if she didn’t ? ”

“ I don’t believe about the white ghost.”

“ Eh, but it be true enough,” said another. “ Why, I used to see the old witch go o’ nights to dig about the Pool-house, and Mas’ Tom Croftly said, when I telled him, that it was to get burned bones to make spells with. I see her night after night, when the stones was smoking still.”

“ Eh, she be witch enough,” said another. “ See how she said that the Pool-house would be blown up some day, and never be builded again. I think she goes with one o’ they owls, as flits about o’ nights.”

“ Shouldn’t wonder,” said the woman with the child ; “ and, if she do screech, see if it bean’t just like they call.”

“ She’ll fly out o’ the fire like one o’ they, see if she don’t, and her wings won’t even be singed. I wonder whether she’ll come back again, and live about here like an owl.

If she do I shan't stay i' this neighb'rood to please nobody, so there."

" Nay, she won't fly away," said one who had not yet spoken. " She'll go down into the earth like, and underneath or into the rocks. Frank Goodsell told me he saw her go right into a solid piece o' rockstone one night as he crossed the forest — she was there one moment, and the next moment she was gone—and became so frighted that he ran away."

" But he ought to ha' searched the place."

" So he did next day, for he was 'shamed o' being scared by an old woman."

" Yes; and what did he see ? "

" Solid stones, and not a hole big enough for a mouse to get into and hide. She just touched the rock with her stick, and it opened and she went in, and it shut up after her. That be a real witch, that be."

" It be a terrifying thing to think of,"

said another. "Only think of going into the earth and stopping for days, like a corpse."

"Nay, but she didn't do that?"

"Eh, but she did, for Frank Goodsell went every day to her cottage to see if she was there, pretending he wanted a charm for a pain in his wife's leg; and he had to go ten days before he found her back, and then she was as quiet and smiling as could be, only she looked white and very terrifying to see."

"Ah, lots of us wondered how she used to live. She'll be back there soon; you see, they'll never get her to burn; and, if they do, she'll harnt the place, and make it bad for everybody. I'm not going to throw a stone at her, poor soul."

"Poor soul, indeed, why she beant got one. She sold it to old what's-his-name long ago."

"Eh, but it be very horrid, said the woman

with the child; and I half wish I had not come to see her burned to death."

" She won't burn."

" Nay," said another, " it be very terrifying; but she'll be dead 'fore they burn her, if they don't be smart. Think of it, though: Mother Goodhugh going to be burned for a witch."

" I don't quite like the old woman to be burnt. How wist she looks !" said the young mother, as she stared at the preparations.

" Hold thy tongue, do," said another; " the country be better without her."

" Ay, it was time something was done now the holy father's gone, and Parson Peasegood won't do naught to exorcise the witch."

" You went to him, didn't a ?"

" Ay, I went to him and told him o' Mother Goodhugh's doings, and how she put a spell on our cow, and evil-wished neighbour Lewin's boy."

" What did he say ? "

" Laughed at me and puffed smoke in my face. ' Go to,' says he, ' for a fool. Thou must get some one to sew some more buttons on thee. Mother Goodhugh be no witch.' "

" Did he say that ? "

" Ay, that he did, and when Betsy Good-sell saw the white sperrit o' Sweet Mace, in the wood near the high rocks and went and asked parson to lay it, he got in such a rage that Betsy had to go."

" She should ha' took him an offering and then he would."

" She did. She took him a two-pound lump o' the fresh butter from her cow after putting a lump o' salt i' the churn to keep out the witch, and told him what she wanted done, and he ups with the butter and throws it at her, and it stuck on the door-post till

Mistress Hilberry come and took it off; and when she heard what was wanted she said Parson ought to do it, and then he called her a silly fool."

" What did she want Parson to do ? "

" To do, why, to lay the spirit that kept walking uneasily night after night. Ay, and it keeps walking now, as a dozen Roehurst folk could tell, only they won't speak about it for fear of doing themselves ill."

" What did Betsy want him to do ? "

" Why, just go and cut a piece o' turf off her grave about a hand-breadth long and a hand-breadth wide, and lay it on the holy table in the church, and after that be done the spirit rests and doesn't trouble people any more."

" He might ha' done that," said the young mother. " I should say it would be wise to get a bit off Mother Goodhugh's grave by-and-by to keep her from walking."

" Eh, but you'll never find grass grow

upon her grave, lass. It will always be black and scathed like."

"Nay, they'll never bury her in no grave. She'll be scattered in dust and ashes to the four winds o' heaven."

"Or the other place," said one of the women, sententiously, and then they all watched the preparations.

"Hush! Look!" cried the young mother in an excited whisper; and a strange murmur ran through the crowd as, at a sign from Sir Thomas, whose florid face was blanched, and blotched with livid patches, a man ran into the cottage with a rough torch.

Master Peasegood saw that the end had come, and, pressing against the pile of faggots which reached up round the victim's neck, he reached over one hand and touched her cheek.

"Courage, poor soul!" he cried earnestly. "Pray with me for mercy in that other land."

The wretched woman seemed to be brought back by the parson's voice, and she stared at him in a curiously dazed manner, her lips moving at last in a whisper that could not be heard.

"Pray with me, my poor soul—let us pray," cried Master Peasegood eagerly.

"No," she said sharply. "It be too late. I want to do some good before I die."

"And it is too late for that," said Master Peasegood to himself, as the excited murmur of the crowd went on.

"No, not to do—to say something, Master—and—and it seems all gone. Yes; I know," she cried, striving hard to hold up her head, which fell back again heavily upon her chest. "No, I can't remember. Yes, Mace, come here, child. I'll give thee to thy father now."

"Poor soul, she wanders," muttered Master Peasegood. Then aloud :— "Try to pray with me, mother. Try—one word."

" Yes, I was not a witch, master.　It was only —— Where be Jeremiah Cobbe ? Here, let me tell him—quick."

" He cannot reach thee now, poor soul.　Pray with me quickly.　Oh, Father have —— "

" Mace.　Here—quick, child, come.　Poor sweet—I had to fight hard to hate thee. My head—my head."

Master Peasegood stretched out a hand to try and sustain the palsied head.

" Stand back, sir," cried Sir Mark fierce-ly ; and he laid his hand upon Master Peasegood's arm, but the stout cleric shook him off.

" Back yourself, sir," he cried, " an' you would not singe your gaudy plumes.　My place is here."

Sir Mark stood back, for at that moment the smoking, flaming torch was thrust into the brushwood, which began to crackle and burn furiously, while a pillar of smoke rose high in the still autumn air, in company with a shriek from the women, some of whom turned away, while others covered their faces with their hands.

The torch was thrust into the faggots again and again, four times in all, and at each thrust there was a burst of flame and a cloud of smoke ; but Master Peasegood stirred not, though the flames licked his long black garb.

The torch-bearer then rose up, and was in the act of thrusting his light right in the centre of the pile, when a strong hand seized it, wrenched it from his hand, and hurled it, as the man staggered back, full in the face of Sir Mark.

A loud chirping whistle rang out at the same moment, and a score of the rough country fellows in long gaberdines, who had been so busy in helping, now took advantage of their forward position to seize the burning faggots and hurl them furiously at the armed men.

Almost before the crowd could realise what was taking place, the flaming brushwood was scattered far and wide, and amidst the smoke a tall, bronzed fellow was seen cutting Mother Goodhugh free.

"Take her, Wat; she's as light as any child," he cried, in a clear voice. "Lead on, we'll cover you."

"Down with them!" shouted Sir Mark, as he recovered from his astonishment; and, drawing his sword, he made a rush at the disturbers of the judicial tragedy.

His first attempt, though, was unfortunate, for he fell over the prostrate body of Master Peasegood, who had been overset in the struggle; and his men hung back as they saw the rough-looking countrymen whip out the weapons they had concealed beneath their gaberdines, and form a bold front.

There was ample room, for the crowd fled shrieking as the bright steel flashed before their eyes. They had gazed in a stupefied, puzzled manner at the disturbance of the faggot pile, and wondered whether it was part of the show or the result of witchcraft; but the bold rescue of the wretched woman they could understand, and they hastened to find safety in flight.

Sir Mark was not long in recovering him-self, and, calling to the armed men to follow, he pursued the retiring party, which retreated steadily along the narrow track, which, after it had passed Mother Goodhugh's, gradually assumed the nature of a forest footpath, and grew more rugged at every step.

Attempts were made to outflank the party, but the density of the forest rendered that impossible, and those who left the path lost ground, while Sir Mark found himself kept at bay by the rear-guard of the retreating men.

"These are no countrymen," he muttered

to himself, as he saw how steadily they kept up the retreat ; and he was in the act of cheering on his little force to make a rush where the pathway opened a little, when cries from behind warned him that he was attacked in the rear.

He bit his lip angrily as he found how cleverly his men were trapped, for it was evident enough that a portion of those he pursued had turned off to right or left, allowing him and his men to pass, and then closing up to attack, this rear movement being the signal for those in front to turn and make a desperate charge upon him and his London men.

It was so sharp a surprise that, at the end of five minutes' cutting and thrusting, Sir Mark was down, faint and sick from a slash across the cheek, and his men had thrown up their weapons and fled helter-skelter through the forest, leaving the rescuers of Mother Goodhugh to proceed in peace.

"Single file, my lads, and away!" cried a well-known voice. "One of you relieve Wat Kilby, and change and change as you grow fagged. Wat, go round by the lower stream. I'll come last and hide the trail."

It required little hiding, for the men passed on and disturbed the herbage but slightly, while, after turning off to right and left in various narrow half-hidden tracks, their course could not have been discovered by the keenest eye, especially as one cut was made right across the forest.

Not a word was spoken, and the roughly-clad, brown-faced men went steadily on. Their load was changed from time to time, and after a while a stoppage was made by a stream, where Mother Goodhugh's face was bathed, and the leader, whom it would have puzzled his best friends to have taken for Gilbert Carr, knelt beside her, and poured a few drops of spirits between her lips.

"Think she's burned, captain?" said a

rough voice that could be none other than that of Wat Kilby.

"No," was the reply, "but I fear we were too late. She will hardly live to our journey's end. Forward, my lads, forward! Did anyone see aught of Master Cobbe?"

"I saw him turn away and go behind the cart," said one of the men. "He was not in the fight."

"And Master Peasegood?"

"I helped him up, captain, and he staggered to the bank, and sat down on a half-burned faggot."

"Then they are all right," said the captain, musingly. "Wat, we shall have to be off to sea again at once. This affair will make the country too hot to hold us."

"Why did you do it then?" growled the old man, gruffly, as he limped along, his scarred face shining in the sun. "She was no good, and will only curse us for our pains."

"Well, Wat," said the captain, sadly,

" and if she does, we can bear another curse or too."

" Ay, or a hundred," was the reply.

It was a hot walk, through the still woods and over streams and ravine-scored hills. The men, as they grew heated, stripped off their rough country Saxon gaberdines, and appeared as light, active seamen of the time, one and all taking turns in carrying Mother Goodhugh, for whom a rough kind of hurdle had been hastily twisted together, and upon it she was laid.

At last the little party was ascending one rugged side of the valley where Anne Beckley had been left to wait the coming of her lover; and after a weary climb the men all had a rest, seating themselves by the spring that gushed from the rocks where the ferns and mosses hung, and after tempering the clear fluid with spirit they began to smoke.

" Let her rest for a time," said Gil; " there

is no danger here. Poor soul! A narrow escape from death." As he spoke he covered the wretched creature with a cloak, and placed a doubled gaberdine beneath her head.

He again trickled a few drops of spirits between the cracked white lips; and, after watching its effects, he rose from his knees, leaving Wat Kilby to fill his little pipe.

"Not much of a job after a twelvemonths' cruise," muttered Wat, as he limped uneasily up and down, "but better than leaving the poor old lass to burn. She's too old and ugly, or she might have done; for I want a wife. Bah! No. She wouldn't do. She's not the witch I want. Eh! captain, did you call?"

"Yes," was the reply; and, on rising, the old lieutenant scrambled up to where Gil, who looked bronzed and ten years older, stood pointing to the stones at the mouth of the store.

"Not been touched, eh, skipper?" said the old fellow.

"No; not by anything more than a rabbit," said Gil, in a grave, quiet voice. "Get up the bars when the lads are rested. We shall have to stay here for the night."

CHAPTER XIV.

HOW WAT KILBY FIRED A TRAIN AND MOTHER GOODHUGH SPOKE.

GIL sat down beside the old woman and remained thinking of what had taken place during the past year. He had sailed away, reckless and heartbroken, caring little where he went, and, after discharging cargo in one of the Spanish ports, he had taken in provisions, and, his men rather welcoming the change, he had made sail for the far East, touching at Ceylon; then on to the Eastern Islands, the lands of spices and strange growths. It was an aimless voyage, but they took in small articles of cargo—silk here, rice there, and dye-woods; and then sailing

further went north and east to China and
Japan, before the vessel's stem was turned
once more for home.

For a strange sense of longing had come
over Gil Carr. Months back he had felt
that he could never see Rochurst more.
Then came the change, with its longing
void in his heart. Night and day it was
ever the same. There was the old place
before his eyes, and a something tugging at
his heartstrings to draw him back. The
face of Sweet Mace seemed gazing appealingly in his as it asked him to come and
save her.

"Save her—from what?" he cried passionately, as he paced up and down the little
deck, looking wild-eyed and strange, while his
men whispered the one to the other, and he
set his teeth firmly and his eyes flashed with
anger, for he knew they thought him mad.

It was the work of a minute almost. They
were sailing into a fresh port in Japan,

where they could see the strangely-dressed people staring at the new comers from the decks of their junks, when Gil suddenly gave orders—he recalled it all—orders to 'bout ship, and they were obeyed without a word.

It was not until they had been sailing on for days that Wat Kilby had come to him with the gruff question, " Where to now, skipper ? "

" *Home !* " was the single word spoken in reply ; and then, as he stood gazing straight before him at the wide expanse of ocean, there arose from the crew a tremendous cheer.

He recalled it all—how he had stood gazing there while order after order was given by Wat Kilby ; how sail after sail had been set and the little vessel careened to the breeze ; while ever before him, with a smile upon her face, the figure of Mace seemed to stand waving him on.

And so it had been during the homeward voyage. Every sail the vessel would bear had been kept set, and she seemed to skim over the sea in fair weather, and to battle bravely in foul, to get back to the little river and her ancient moorings beneath the trees.

He recalled telling himself that he was mad, for this was but another phase of his humour. But a short time back he was restless to get farther and farther away; now he had conjured up this phantasy to call him back—back to what?

A bitter sob would struggle from his heart as he told himself it was to gaze again upon poor Mace's grave.

Always there, sleeping or waking, never shut from his mental vision, that sweet, pale face smiling at him as the ship sped on; and only when forced by want of provisions did they enter port, till once more upon the tide the weather-beaten ship rode safely into the mouth of the little river. Then the big boat was lowered and manned, a tow-rope run out, and the men pulled cheerily to keep the little vessel's head straight as she glided on up the fast narrowing stream, till the spars nearly touched the branches on either side, and her old moorings were made.

Wat Kilby played the part of spy, and went ashore, for now that they were back the fancy that had floated before Gil's eyes had been seen no more; and moody and despondent he had shrunk from leaving his ship.

It was Wat Kilby then who made his way over the hills and through the forest to the village, and had borne back the news which stirred Gil to action; and for Mace's sake, as he said, he had determined to save poor old Mother Goodhugh from so horrible a fate.

" She would have urged me to do it," he said to himself; and, making his plans, he had been successful; while there, half dead, the poor creature lay, with the adventurer sitting meditating by her side.

"What shall I do now?" said Gil to himself in a bitter tone. "Set sail again, I suppose, for this Sir Mark, unless too busy with his wedding, will try to hunt us down.

"Well, let him come if he will," he added, wearily, and then rising. "Now, my lads!" he cried, "to work."

His men jumped up; and as he stood by, watching and thinking how in one year the ferns and wild plants set in the crevices had concealed the mouth of the store, iron bars and shovels were plied, the stones loosened and thrown aside, till at last only one large piece remained, and that had so tightly wedged itself in that it resisted all their efforts to dislodge it.

"Come boys," Wat Kilby cried, "have you left all your strength in the Indies? Lay to at it with a will. Now, all together —heave ho!"

As he spoke he brought his whole strength to bear upon it, but dropped the bar directly after, and stood shaking his head; for he had never recovered from the terrible burns and injuries he had received at the explosion—injuries that had left him for months a helpless invalid during the early part of the voyage, and a cripple for life.

"Skipper," he said, "I'm not quite so strong as I was, and my bones don't seem to be knit together as they were. It'll take some pounds o' Mas' Cobbe's best to lift that out."

Gil frowned, for the old man's speech brought up a host of painful recollections.

"Shall we get up some powder, skipper?" said Wat.

"And fire the barrels that are in the store?" said Gil sternly.

"Nay," growled the old fellow; "we could hoist out that stone without reaching any that is in yonder: it is too far away."

" Get it then," said Gil indifferently ; and a couple of men were despatched to the ship, returning after some two or three hours with the keg, which they carried in turn.

Mother Goodhugh had not moved, but lay in a kind of stupor with half-closed eyes, Gil sitting near and dreaming over the past.

A slight rustle near him made him gaze upwards once to see a rabbit scurry away from a hole beneath the great stone, and this he marked as suitable for laying the charge to lift away the mass.

At last, the men came toiling up the steep ascent, and Wat Kilby busied himself in preparing a mine that should do what was required without further damage to the store.

It was soon done—a train laid, and a fuse prepared. Then Mother Goodhugh was carefully lifted and laid behind a corner of the rock, where harm could not befall her, and Wat Kilby stood ready to fire the fuse after seeing all the men were safe.

"Now, captain," he said, "as soon as you like."

"Stop a moment," said Gil, thoughtfully, though all the time he was experiencing a fierce longing to enter the cave once more.

"What for, captain?" said Wat gruffly, as he puffed at his pipe.

"The sound may be heard, and bring Sir Mark's fellows down."

"Nay," cried Wat, "the noise will run down the valley and out to sea, my lad. They'll not hear it inland, I lay my life. Bah! and if they did, what then? No one could find his way here without a guide."

"Go on, then," said Gil quietly; and, drawing back to the shelter of a little recess, he stood watching the acts of Wat Kilby, a famous old gunner in his way, as, after puffing at his pipe to make it glow, he just touched the end of the fuse, laid the other end by the train, and limped coolly to the captain's side.

From the rocky recess they could see the fuse sparkle and burn rapidly away, and listen to the buzz of the voices of the crew as they talked of the explosion; then a zig-zag line of fire seemed to run along amongst the heather and ferns; there was a blinding flash, a thick white smoke, and, lastly, a heavy dull roar that rolled down the ravine, and the fall of masses of the splintered rock.

The smoke rose slowly over the face of the cliff, showing the grey and blackened traces where the fire had blasted bush and tree; while, where the large block of sand-stone had lain was now a dark opening, the rock having been lifted right away, reft in twain, and thrown some yards down the slope.

" There, skipper," growled Wat, as he limped along, and the men came up;

" there be not a cask split inside I'll wager, and a few showers of rain will hide all the marks."

Gil nodded.

" Four of you bring the old woman along," he said. " We'll make her a bed inside. Good God !"

He was startled at what he saw, for the explosion seemed to have roused Mother Goodhugh, who came crawling painfully towards them to raise herself upon her knees and point, and struggle to speak.

" Yes, yes," she cried. " Powder, powder —the cursed stuff. Cobbe's work; Cobbe's work. He slew my dear with it, and now— ha, ha, ha ! I have brought it home to him. Listen, boy, come here."

Gil stepped to her side, and she clutched at his wrist, and clung to it, as she turned her ashy, distorted face to him, but only for it to droop back upon her chest so that she gazed at him in a way that was horribly grotesque.

"Listen; do you hear. She wanted it stopped—that wedding—Mistress Anne—the jealous fool, and paid me for it all. I did— I stopped it. Do you hear? I got the key —the powder-cellar, and laid a train—a long, long, train all the way to the cellar, and hid myself in the garden—there safe away. Do you see? just down yonder," she panted, pointing to the part of the ravine from which she had crawled.

"I did it—I did it. I waited hours and hours till you came by me—all of you, and began to fight with Sir Mark's men—and then I struck with my flint and steel—and the fire —ran along the ground—and the powder blew up as it did when I lost my dear, and—and —why is it daylight? Why does the sun shine?" she continued, gazing wildly from one to the other.

"She's daft," growled Wat. "Poor soul! they have frightened away her wits."

"Silence," cried Gil. "Let her speak."

"Who says I'm daft?" cried Mother Goodhugh, gathering strength. "I am not; but I know, I know. Ha, ha, ha! I wanted to stop the wedding and make my words come true. It was a judgment, too, on Mas' Jeremiah Cobbe, and I fired his powder-store."

"She thinks it is a year ago," muttered Gil, gazing at her with horror.

"Yes, yes. I've had my revenge," muttered the old woman, gazing round wildly, as she struggled to keep her head erect, "and burnt his place. He has paid me now for my dearies, whom he killed. Poor souls! poor souls! One so white and cold when they drew him from the water; the other so blackened and so burned. But she was not so burned. Poor child! poor child! poor child!"

" Mother Goodhugh," cried Gil hoarsely, " did you fire the Pool-house ?"

" Yes, yes, yes; the powder," gibbered the old woman, as she dragged her head up, and it once more fell back upon her chest. " I did it well; and now I'll forgive him. I'll curse Mas' Cobbe no more. I did it just now. You heard it roar. See, it has burned my hands—my hair, but never mind; I've had revenge."

" Then it was you who fired the powder there—that dreadful night," cried Gil furiously, as he clutched the weak old creature by the throat.

" Yes, I did it," chuckled the old woman; then, throwing up her hands as if in pain— " but Sweet Mace—poor Sweet Mace—they thought it killed her, too. I hated her; and yet, no; she was very good and sweet. I saw him bring her out— yes, it was you— and laid her—dead upon the ground. Yes, I saw; and she turned to a white spirit—yes, white spirit—and she comes to see me—no: does she?—I can't think—it was just now I got her out, and she has come to me ever since, so white and sad, and she looks at me always with her great soft eyes. Poor child! poor girl! I've wept about her sore, for she was as good and gentle as Mistress Anne was bad."

The spirit was in Gil Carr to strangle the old woman as she made her hideous confession, but her words of pity for sweet Mace disarmed him, and he let her sink to the earth, where she crouched, gazing feebly from one to the other, and fighting hard to sustain her tottering head.

"Yes, yes, yes," she moaned piteously; "she comes looking so white and sad to ask me why I killed her, and it makes my heart so sore. But I shall bring her to her senses again some day, perhaps—some day. Hush, hush! not a word. If you speak she goes again. There—there—look, look!" cried the old woman in a hoarse whisper, as, throwing one arm round Gil's leg, she leaned her head against it, steadied herself, and pointed with her skinny fingers. "Yes, there she be. Poor child! poor child! Mace, child, I did not mean to harm thee. Wilt forgive me, dear? See! see!"

As she pointed they glanced in the direction indicated by the old woman's finger, and Gil uttered a cry, for in the dark, powder-riven entry to the store, and not a dozen yards away, stood a weird figure with long, flowing hair. The arms and shoulders were bare, and the white hands covered the face, giving it as it stood in the obscurity of the cave a spiritual look that made even the least superstitious of the party—Gil himself —shudder, feeling that he was in the presence of a being of another world.

CHAPTER XV.

HOW CULVERIN CARR SOLVED A PROBLEM.

SWEET MACE stood motionless in the opening, a soft blue reek floating gently out from the store, as the damp air of the place was driven forth by a downward current through a fissure far in its depths; and this, as it surrounded the rescued prisoner, added to the unreality of the scene. For the figure was seen through a medium that rendered it unsubstantial in aspect, added to which the deadly whiteness of the brow and hands made it look unnatural to a degree.

For some time no one spoke. The men grouped together, stared at the strange apparition in the cavern mouth, and Wat Kilby gazed from it to his leader and back, while the soft wind wafted the blue haze from the opening away from the motionless figure, and then enveloped it again, as if it were part and parcel of the subterranean abode, and it sought to draw its occupant back to its shades.

Mother Goodhugh was the first to break the silence, as, crawling towards the place on hands and knees, she crouched at last at Mace's feet, and lay there, panting.

" She has come from the dead to fetch me," moaned the old woman, whose reason seemed to wander. " I know her. See how white, and cold, and strange she is. My child, my child, I killed thee, I killed thee; and now—now—have pity on me! have pity! I be not a witch."

She grovelled lower and lower, clasping Mace's bare, white feet, and laid her cheek against them, while, still keeping one hand across her eyes, the poor girl bent down slowly, and touched the crouching wretch.

Gil had remained motionless till now; but as he saw the figure move, his faith in its being supernatural was shaken, and with a loud cry he ran forward with outstretched hands.

"Mace," he cried, hoarsely, "speak to me, oh, speak!"

He had not touched her, for in his surprise it seemed possible, after Mother Goodhugh's words, that the woman he loved had come back from the dead, but still his common sense revolted, while his eyes asserted that it was true.

As he spoke Mace rose upright again, but without removing her hand from her eyes, and Gil saw that her long hair was grey as that of some venerable dame; that the slight garment she wore was ragged, and that her fingers were torn and bleeding fast.

He could not tell what it meant; how she came to be there; but the idea of the supernatural was cleared away, and, making an effort over his slavish dread, he caught the disengaged hand in his.

It was like ice, but his touch broke the spell, for, with a piteous cry, Mace tottered and would have fallen had not Gil caught her in his arms.

She was deathly cold, and as he bore her to a spot where the soft turf was dotted with purple heather he saw that her eyelids were tightly closed, and her brow knit as if with pain; and, judging that the glow of sunshine caused her to suffer, he laid a kerchief across her eyes before clasping her icy hands and trickling a few drops of water between her lips.

A host of confusing thoughts rushed through his brain, the only substantial one he could grasp being that Mace must have gone to the cavern to seek him, and then have been shut in.

But this idea was driven away on the instant by an older recollection, one which made him groan in the anguish of his heart.

" My love is dead," he panted. " Did not these hands lay her in her grave ? God in heaven have mercy on me! Am I going mad ? "

" Skipper," whispered a voice at his side, and looking up he saw old Wat standing with dilated eyes, pointing down at the insensible figure. " Skipper," the old fellow whispered hoarsely, " we bean't cowards, but the old woman be a witch after all. Come away, come away! "

In his strange confusion of mind, Gil was for the moment ready to accept this theory, and he gazed down at the weird figure beside him, and then at Mother Goodhugh, where she lay. Was there really truth then in witchcraft, and had this old woman the power to recall the dead ?

He looked at the deathly white face, the white hair, then at the cave mouth, and the surroundings of the bright sunlit ravine, and his group of wonder-stricken men, and then his every-day common sense prevailed. It was no myth, no trick of witchcraft, but a living, breathing form. It was Mace, the dead restored, his lost love, she whom he had mourned. How it was he did not know, neither could he stop to consider while she lay helpless by his side. Mace lived again, and the mystery must rest.

"Wat," he cried, as like a flash of lightning the thought entered his brain. "The dead — the grave—it was Janet who was killed."

The old man shook his head, but Gil paid no heed, for a low sigh had just escaped from Mace's lips, and, bending down, he raised her head upon his arm, swept aside her long grey hair, and kissed her stony brow.

It was enough for him that she lived — that she whom he had mourned was restored to him, and raising the kerchief slightly he gazed in silent wonderment at the fast-closed eyes.

Then he awoke to the fact that it was time for action, and not for wonder, and rousing himself he began to give orders.

"Quick, my lads," he cried; "make up a couch of the sailcloth in yonder, and carry in yon poor old creature. Wat, have a fire lit, then cut some of the ling, and make another couch."

Their leader's words broke the spell that seemed to have charmed the men, who hurriedly obeyed, while Gil strove hard to restore the icy frame he held to consciousness, trembling lest the shock had been too severe, and fighting hard to keep his brain from dwelling upon the mystery.

" Dead ! " whispered a voice at his ear, and a pang shot through his breast as he gazed in horror at the face resting against his heart.

" No ! " he cried hoarsely. " Dog ! you lie "

" No, no, skipper : the old witch—Mother Goodhugh. She be gone."

" Art sure ? " cried Gil, with a sigh of relief.

" Sartain, skipper. She was almost gone before."

" Heaven forgive her ! " said Gil, softly. " Wat, lay her decently in the furthest part of the store till we can put her to rest. See that a couch is ready. Poor sweet ! she cannot bear the light."

As he spoke, handling her as tenderly as if she had been an infant, Gil rose up and bore the insensible girl into the store, where the state of the objects around told him plainly that she must have been a prisoner for months.

In a few minutes' time he had her lying upon a bed of soft heather, softened with a sail and a couple of heavy cloaks for cover-lids, as he sought to infuse warmth, and with it life.

As evening came on, Gil knelt beside the motionless figure upon the rough couch, in an agony of spirit, for, in spite of all his efforts, Mace seemed to be slipping away from him once again.

He had fancied that the marble coldness that had struck a chill to his heart was not so marked, but he could not be sure; and at last, after trickling spirits between the white lips, and trying all he could to promote warmth, he knelt there waiting despairingly for the result.

The sun had descended beyond the hills, turning the far west into one blaze of mellow

golden glory; there was a faint twittering
from the linnets and finches that hung about
the bushes on the steep slopes and crags;
and on one rugged old hawthorn, whose
roots were thrust amongst the rifts and crags
of the sandstone, a solitary thrush was sing-
ing his evening hymn.

As Gil watched the face of her who lay
there as rigid almost as if in death, it
seemed to him that the soft sweet face that
looked so smooth and young, and yet so old,
was not so ashy white as a short time before;
but directly after he realised the fact that
the warm sunset flush was reflected into the
store, and with a groan of despair he bent
down and kissed the cold lips, and tried to
breathe into the icy frame the vigour that
throbbed and bounded in every nerve and
vein of his own.

But no: there was no movement, and at
last, when Wat Kilby came softly up to say
that one of the look-out men had encountered

a Roehurst founder, and learned from him that Sir Mark and Mistress Anne were married and gone away, and that there was no pursuit, Gil bade him sternly begone, for he muttered :

" The old wound is torn asunder, and I must seek for consolation with the dead."

That she might live was Gil's prayer ; that, if a victim were needed to offer up to death, his own poor worthless life might be taken. For it was agony indeed. He had begun to carry his load of misery with patient resignation, and had been content to revisit the spots where so many happy hours had been spent ; but to come back to this was more than he could bear.

The warm glow of the setting sun died out, to leave all ashy grey, and in mute despair Gil gazed down upon the white, rigid face before him. How cold she was, and how changed ! Her silver hair, as it lay dishevelled around, formed a soft halo about the placid face, for the contraction of the brow had passed away, and, with the fading of the light, the drawn and pained expression of the eyelids had given place to a peaceful look that inspired him with awe. While though at times he fancied that she breathed, it was so faintly that he could not be sure, the icy coldness seemed to increase.

As the night drew on Gil knew it was impossible to get help, and in his despair he felt that he could only wait and hope. His men, saving those who watched, contrived themselves a rough tent under the shelter of the over-hanging rock, and at last, as the fire they had made died out, Gil knelt there alone with her who had been his boyhood's love, his manhood's deepest passion, and, feeling that she was gliding from him once again, he flung himself by her side, clasped the icy form to his breast, and sought by his despairing kisses to win from it some token of life.

It was in vain, and the warmth he sought to impart fled from his own breast to receive back the icy chill from hers.

The night stole on, and the soft whispers from the forest around were heard from time to time, or a withered leaf fell with a noise that was striking in the stillness around. Sometimes an owl swept past the cavern's mouth on ghostly wing, making its presence known by its strange cry. The stars glittered and blinked and shed their soft light, while from time to time a faint breeze from the sea swept through the forest and up the glade, where it sighed and seemed to sob as it appeared to enter the cavern, and then fled shivering away.

Now and again some muttered word or uneasy motion on the part of one of the men could be heard, and at stated times the gaunt form of Wat Kilby was seen to go limping past, as he changed his sentries. Then the hours slipped by, and Gil still lay there clasping the senseless form to his breast—the form of the dead he told himself again and again, till utterly worn out with grief and despair a stupor more than a sleep fell upon him, and the present passed away.

It was broad daylight, and a faint flush of the coming sunshine was reflected from the side of the ravine visible from where Gil lay, while for a few moments he could not collect his thoughts. There was a strange buoyant feeling in his breast to which it had long been a stranger, and he lay wondering what it meant, till, like a flood, the recollection of the past night came upon him, and with a groan he turned his eyes to gaze upon the sweet, dead face of her he loved; but only to start up on his elbow, trembling with dread lest he should have been deceived.

For it was no icy marble frame that he had clasped to his breast. The warm life-blood of his heart had seemed to communicate its vitality to her who lay insensible there, and sent the current of life, that month by month had grown more sluggish in its course, bounding through artery and vein once more; and, as he bent lower and lower, it was to feel Mace's soft, warm breath upon his cheeks.

He caught her hand in his and placed it on his breast. It was icy cold, but it was not deathly; and, when in a passion of thankfulness and joy he rained his kisses on brow and lips, the clammy, rigid feeling had quite passed away.

He knew that she lived; but there was no reply to his caresses. Asleep or in a strange stupor, he could not tell which; but as he released her she lay back motionless, save that her breast heaved softly, and her breathing was regular and slow.

He spoke to her with his lips to her ear, but there was no reply; he raised her in his arms and gazed in her pale face, but still there was no response; and, trembling lest she should again slip from him, he softly laid her head upon the rough pillow and tried to think of some plan to fan the tiny spark of life into a warmer glow.

Rousing his followers, and regardless now of discovery, so that he could gain help, Gil despatched Wat Kilby to Roehurst, and others to the ship and the nearest town, the result being, that the same evening the insensible girl was carefully borne to Croftley's cottage, near her ruined home.

CHAPTER XVI.

HOW SWEET MACE AWAKENED ON HER WEDDING-DAY.

A SENSATION of intense heat. Then a feeling as if her head were on fire, followed by a terrible pain.

How long this lasted Mace never knew, but she lay there confused and troubled. One feeling, however, was dominant. It was very nearly the time when Gil would be beneath the window, and she must take off that wedding dress, and send her maid away.

What a mockery it was, that dress, and how hot and clammy it seemed. She shuddered in one of her more lucid moments, as it struck her that it was like a winding-sheet, and she recalled that she had often wished herself dead.

How dark it was, and how steaming and hot. Drip, drip, drip, drip. The noise of dripping water, every drip seemed as if it struck upon her brain, and caused her suffering. Why, it rained!

Well, what matter? What was rain to Gil, who, in his frail ship, dared the greatest storms that blew?

He would come, let the weather be what it might.

Then she seemed to be overcome with sleep, to awake once more with the pain less and her head clearer.

Drip, drip, drip. The rain still falling, and she felt, in a helpless way, that she must have been to sleep again, and began to wonder how long Gil would be.

It was still intensely dark, and very close

and stifling, the heat seemed to be more than she could bear.

How long would Gil be? Poor fellow, how cruelly he must have felt it to hear that she was to wed another, and—yes. Why, had not Janet taken off the wedding dress before she lay down to sleep.

How bad her head had been. She never remembered to have suffered such pains before; and then that terrible thirst! How horribly she had dreamed, too. She recollected now; a horrible dream. First, Gil had clasped her in his arms; then it was not Gil, but Sir Mark; and even now she shuddered at the thoughts of the grim shade which had come next.

But it was a dream consequent upon the excitement she had gone through; and now she had awakened, and it must be time for Gil to be beneath her window.

She did not attempt to rise, for the strange feeling of stupor still held her, and she lay quite still, till the thought that she might have slept too long came and sent a thrill through her brain, and she started up to listen, becoming conscious of a strange, suffocating odour as of dank, hot mist.

How black it was! She could not see the window, and, with the confused sensation of one waking in the darkness, she sat gazing about and listening.

Still that ceaseless drip, drip, drip, of water, but the gurgle of the water-pipe that went down by the side of the gable was not there, and it suddenly struck her that she could not hear the familiar rushing noise of the race, where the water hurried towards the wheel.

She stretched out her hand to rise from the bed, and it touched something rough and hard, making her withdraw it, but only to stretch it forth again and find that she was touching wood and roughened stone.

"Where am I?" she said, softly; and as

she spoke she made out tiny sparks of light.

"Gil's signals!" she cried. "But why does he show them now?"

She tried to get off the bed, but no bed was there; and, after feeling about for a few minutes, she clasped her hands to her head.

"What does this terrible silence mean?" she faltered. "Where am I? Where is Gil?"

There was the slow drip of the water for answer—nothing more; and she tried to recall the past.

"I have been to sleep," she said, "heavily asleep: and yet I don't know."

She tried to collect her thoughts, but seemed to grow more confused.

"I must have been very ill," she said, at last. "And it began directly I had drunk of that water. But how long is it ago? And why is it so dark? Where am I?

Weak and prostrated by the terrible shock

she had suffered, a curious sensation of stupor overcame her once more, and she crouched down to save herself from falling, as she dropped into a feverish sleep.

When she awoke again her head was clearer, but she was terribly weak. It was dark as ever, but the suffocating feeling had gone, and she could no longer see the signal lights, but the peculiar drip, drip, of water was there.

" I must have slept again long past the time when Gil would come," she said, with a wild feeling of yearning for him; and now again she tried to make out where she was.

" I must be mad!" she exclaimed in a despairing tone, and she started, for her voice seemed followed by a hollow whispering murmur, that sent a shudder through her frame.

Crouching down once more, she waited with eyes and ears on the strain, but still there was nothing to be seen, no sound to be heard but that ceaseless drip, drip of water that fell with a faint musical plash somewhere hard by.

But her senses were gradually growing clearer, her perceptions more vivid, and she tried to make out what was the meaning of a peculiar heavy odour.

"It is powder!" she exclaimed, with a shudder. "Can there have been a mishap while I slept?"

She paused, trying to think, and her senses grew clearer still.

"Yes, it is powder; there must have been an explosion;" and she recalled the strange, dank, pungent odour that she had often breathed when some accident had occurred.

"But when? How could the powder have fired?"

She tried hard to think it out: but her mind was still too confused, and in a helpless manner she groped her way in the direction of the dropping water, till she felt a splash upon her head, and, stooping down, plunged her hands into what seemed to be a deep, cold pool.

With the avidity of one perishing from thirst, she scooped up the water and drank again and again, each draft she took seeming to infuse new life within her veins; and, at last satisfied, she tried to master the horrible feeling of dread that was overpowering her, and to make out her position.

" Let me go back," she said, forcing herself to the point. " I will not be alarmed at what is perhaps some trifling accident. Now, then—I went to my bedroom to be ready when Gil should come. I was feverish and thirsty, and I drank from the jug upon my table. Then I grew worse, and Janet came to try on my dress. I must have lain down and had some frightful dream.

" Yes, I remember it now : and I tried

on the dress in a half-stupefied way. Nay,
it must have been Janet as I lay half asleep,
half mad ——

"Oh, God!" she moaned, "am I half
mad now?"

There was a hollow, echoing whisper,
and she cowered there trembling for a time,
but, recovering, she forced herself to go
on.

"I was lying there ill and quite asleep,
and—yes—no—yes—I have some recollection of cries—a terrible shock—and—it
must be—it must be."

She pressed her hands to her head, and
rocked herself to and fro, for her reason
was on the verge of being shattered, so
horrible were her thoughts.

By degrees, though, she grew calmer, and
she once more tried to unravel the mystery
of the thick darkness around, and to carry
this out she again drank from the pool.
Then her hands touched stones and timber;

and at last, after a long struggle, she fully realised the facts. There could be no doubt of it, for she recognised again the peculiar odour of the powder.

This had come while she slept, then, overwhelming her so suddenly that she had not awakened from the stupor in which she was plunged. The powder had exploded, and she must have fallen with the ruins down into the vault where her father had a store.

She made a brave struggle against the feelings that seemed to bear down with overwhelming violence, ready to snatch her reason away, but she was only weak, and at last, with a burst of hysterical sobbing, she sank back completely overcome. It seemed as if the drugged sleep into which she had been plunged by Mother Goodhugh's distilments had returned, for her reason became overclouded, and then all was blank.

It was like awakening once more in the utter darkness that she became conscious of the drip, drip, of the water from the roof, as it fell into the pool that lay somewhere near her feet.

Again she had to fight her way to a knowledge of her position; and now, with her head far clearer, she became fully conscious that this was no dream. The idea of death or madness grew weaker, while that which pointed to some terrible explosion and the destruction of the place gained better hold. The odour of the exploded gunpowder grew so faint as to be scarcely perceptible, but it was still there, and had she wanted further evidence she found it upon touching some of the stones, for her hands were damp and clammy with the reek that would have been black, for she was too well versed in her father's trade not to be certain upon such a point.

There was relief even in this, for in spite of the horrors of her position, this common-sense knowledge relieved her mind of the morbid terrors that had been ready to sweep away her reason, and set her thinking of escape.

The knowledge that she was literally buried alive was almost more than she could bear at times; but, us her brain grew clearer, hope began to dawn life a soft, pale ray amidst the real and mental blackness all around.

There was no doubt now: the Pool-house had been destroyed by a terrible explosion, either of the powder in the cellar stores or by some calamity outside; and, shivering with horror, she gave way for the moment to the superstitious belief that it was a judgment upon her for not having faith that the wedding would be put off. She smiled, though, directly after, at the absurdity of the idea, and began to wonder how those she loved had fared.

Gil? Had he been near the place? And her father, what of him—was he safe? Janet, too, poor girl! She hoped that no ill had overtaken her.

Then she shuddered, for the idea had come upon her that Sir Mark might have suffered, too, and be even now alive or dead within a few yards of where she lay.

In spite of a great effort she could not keep from shrieking aloud at this idea. She crouched listening, almost expecting to hear step or word, and, in place of being ready to welcome them, she was prepared to turn and flee from what, instead of seeming like a companionship, bore the aspect to her of another frightful calamity.

Then, with her mind upon Gil, and the feeling strong that those above must be making a search for her, she felt that she ought to make some efforts to let them know her whereabouts.

She raised her voice, and cried loudly— "Gil—father—help—I am here!" But there was no reply to her wild cry, no sound of iron bar or pick removing some heap of stones, and in spite of her efforts she could do no more than sob as if her heart would break.

And now, as if to give her mental relief from the horrors that she had passed through, came long periods of sleep and dreams of happy times—bright, sunny skies, the waving trees, and flowery meads. Gil was with her, and they were fishing once more upon the lake.

It seemed to be spring-time, the time of love and hope and joy; and in fancy she saw again the waving woods, the silvery bosom of the lake dotted with broad green leaves, waving sedges, and the silver and golden chalices of the lilies starting up from the water as if held out by some pixie's hand. There, too, were the distant hills, and the empurpled heathery waste, where the golden gorse grew so densely. The meadow with its waving grass ready for the scythe. The old garden lush with flowers and advancing fruit. Its round-topped beehives, the pleasant sheltered seats and grassy walks; and then the bright scene seemed, dream-like, to fade away in the rich soft glow of evening, and she was once more at her window gazing, but blushing and happy with expectancy, for there, out on the far green bank, shone the signal lights of four glowworms, and directly after there was a noise, and a voice so deep and clear came up, making her heart beat as it uttered her name.

Yes, there it was; he called her; and with her hands pressed to her heaving bosom she answered him back—

" Yes, yes, Gil—love—I am here."

She started up with straining eyes, so real did it seem, and then sank back sobbing bitterly, for it was but a dream. And so was this noise of falling stones and crackling wood, with the rush as of a mass of broken fragments that had crumbled down beside her—all a dream, from which after three weary days of pain she did not care to make the effort to rouse herself. For the Poolhouse had been destroyed, and she must be dead, even though Mother Goodhugh's voice had come to her, perhaps to curse. For that was Mother Goodhugh calling to her in this dream, bidding her rise and come forth, and live again, and then all was blank.

Blank to Sweet Mace, but no dream, for her cries had been heard by the old woman, as she haunted the ruins by night, picking out little objects of value, and toiling from the first to reach poor forgotten Janet, an object that kept her busy, for she could not rest till that was done. The sixth night had come before she had been able to drag away a sufficiency of the *débris* to reach the imprisoned girl. She had not dared to summon help from the dread she suffered lest Sir Mark's men should seize her once again; and when at last she succeeded in dragging the sufferer from her living tomb, and had laid her upon the ground hard by, there was none to see her in the grey of the early morning staggering with her burden to her lonely cottage in the lane.

CHAPTER XVII.

HOW MOTHER GOODHUGH MISSED HER REVENGE.

"Dead, and they've buried her!" cried the old woman, as she stood beside the bed, whereon she had lain Mace. "Dead, and they've buried her; and Jeremiah Cobbe can feel now what it be to lose one that he loves!"

"Let him feel it," she snarled, "let him feel it, and gnaw his heart for a time. I'll tell him naught."

Then she glanced uneasily at the door, and drew the curtain that screened her bed.

"No one can see her now," she muttered. "I'll keep her as long as I can. She be weak and half-childish with what she has gone through. Let her rest; but I'm glad she be not killed."

A feeling of satisfaction glowed for a time in the old woman's heart, but it was mingled with annoyance that, after all, Jeremiah Cobbe would know rest, while she could never recall her dead.

As the days glided by, to her surprise Mother Goodhugh found that Mace did not recover. She partook of food mechanically when it was offered to her, but she did not speak, only looked vacantly about her, and seemed to be without even the power to think.

" Why should I lose my revenge ? " thought the old woman. " Why should I even let him think that she lives ? It will be another to keep until he finds her out, and that may be months first, if she stops as she be now. But I can keep her easily," she said with a chuckle, " since corn grows on the moonbeams, and meal can be had for all my wants from out the earth."

A month had gone by, and Mace showed no sign of being roused from her dull, apathetic state. She made no attempt to move, but sat where she was placed, gazing straight before her, and never a word passed her lips. Whether the old woman was by her or she was away on some errand, it was all the same, Mace stayed where she was left, unseen by a soul, for since the explosion at the Pool-house no one had cared to go near Mother Goodhugh, and but for her foresight she might have starved.

But the old woman had a means of keeping body and soul together that people little dreamed of, for one day, while herb-gathering in the woodlands, far away behind the founder's house, she had kicked against a fragment of iron, which proved to be a portion of a shell; and, passing further in search of more, she came upon a hole in the sandstone rock beside the scarped mass that rose behind the Pool-house.

Such a place had its interest for her; for, by the fragments of iron about and the blackened appearance of the rock, she could tell that it was the work of one of Jeremiah Cobbe's pieces of ordnance.

Parting the ferns and tangled growth with her stick, and muttering a curse or two upon him and his belongings, the old woman found that there was an opening large enough to pass through; and, investigating further, she could see that the great shell had broken through what was but a thin crust of rock, and that within there was a narrow passage-like opening, worn apparently by the waters of some ancient stream.

Another day she examined further, for the place interested her, and she penetrated some distance and returned.

Another time she came, and brought a lanthorn to search further, for anything bordering on mystery was valuable to her, ending, after winding in and out for some distance, by coming to the conclusion that this was the place of which Abel Churr had spoken—that she had long sought in vain, and that she knew Gil Carr's secret, having hit upon another entrance to his store.

It was a long and tedious way in, but that mattered little to her; while, ignorant of the fact that he had been the means of breaking a way into his own treasure-house, Gil Carr duly, as he believed, sealed it up and set sail.

Here one night, when the fear was upon her that Mace might be discovered at her cottage, and the malignant fit was stronger than usual, Mother Goodhugh brought the helpless girl. A touch of the hand was sufficient to lead her where her gaoler willed, and, docile as a child, Mace accompanied her to what was hereafter to be her prison, whose dark shadows seemed to accord with her helpless state; and here she would sit and seem to doze away her life.

It was a safe place, only visited by the old woman at night, and she found it easy to feed her prisoner from the ship-stores; but now and then a fit of remorse would seize upon her, and she would, on leaving the place, resolve to restore the poor girl to her home.

A dozen times over she threw herself in Jeremiah Cobbe's way to tell him all, but the sight of the founder seemed to raise up gall and bitterness in her heart, and she went away chuckling and laughing.

"Let him suffer a little longer—a little longer," was her cry. "Some day the girl will recover her senses, then I'll speak."

But the time flew by, and sense was as it

were dead in Sweet Mace's brain; while, having gone so far, Mother Goodhugh dreaded at last to bring her back. There were strange rumours afloat about her, and her position was not so safe as it had been of yore. So in utter fear she would fasten up her cottage and take refuge in Gil's store for days together, dreading lest ill should befall her; but at the end of a week passed in this gloomy abode she would be ready to revile herself for her cowardice, and go back. At these times she was more than ever prepared to own that she could not restore Mace to her father.

"Let him suffer, as I have done," she would cry again. "She can stay till Gil Carr comes back. Let him take the poor stricken idiot if he will. I've had revenge, and a sweet one after all."

In this spirit Mother Goodhugh would return to her cottage, and the tale of her evil doings grew longer, for there were those who

said that she disappeared for days together
—none knew where; and that she had always
meal in plenty, while the miller swore none
ever came from him, and that she was a
witch indeed.

CHAPTER XVIII.

HOW CROFTLY CUT THE HAY IN THE TWO-YEAR STACK.

THERE was a great deal of talk about punishing those who had rescued Mother Goodhugh from the flames; but Sir Mark was away with his wife, and soon after his marriage, being somewhat of a favourite of the British Solomon, he was appointed to a diplomatic post at one of the continental courts, and when Sir Thomas Beckley took his first steps to vindicate the insult offered to the law he received so broad a hint that he might suffer bodily for his interference, that he quietly shut himself up in his old house, surrounded by the carp-haunted moat, and took walks upon its bank to give the gaping, staring fish a model that they might study for their benefit at will.

In fact, the rescue of Mother Goodhugh was half forgotten in the news that was spread by the superstitious that by her subsequent death a spell had been broken, and Sweet Mace had been set free and had returned to life.

For by degrees she was restored, but it was only by long and patient nursing. In the latter part of her imprisonment her faculties had become dulled, and the shock had produced a semi-torpid state that had its effect upon her mental powers, which were slow to recover their tone. Gil was ever by her side, though she did not know him or her father; but, after a month's prostration, during which she had hardly left her couch, she began to fight her way very slowly back to strength.

Tender nursing prevailed, and, could her health, drunk in flagons of ale, have given it back sooner, Master Peasegood would have insured her the most robust of constitutions months before she was seated in the old garden, an object of curiosity to all who saw her, with the face of twenty and the silvery hair of three-score and ten.

But the ashy pallor gave way to the returning hue of health, and the rigid, fixed features became softened and rounded. It was Sweet Mace's old face again by the next summer, all but a couple of deeply-marked lines in her forehead—lines of care and thought which still remained.

The founder sighed even in his joy at her return, for still there was something wanting.

"Nay, Gil," he said, sadly, "thou hast brought me back the body of my darling, but thou hast not brought the spirit. She smiles sadly and gazes at me when I speak, and that is all."

" Yes, that is all," groaned Gil; " she knows me no longer."

" Poor lad, poor lad ! " muttered Master Peasegood, who was present ; and he drowned his sigh in a flagon of ale.

" Art going to rebuild the old house, now ? " said the parson.

" Ay," said the founder, " and at once. I have my hopes that the sight of the old place, made as near like as can be, even to the trees, may do the poor child good, for she seems at her best when I take her round the garden."

Gil looked up curiously, for a thought had struck him ; but he said nothing ; and, on the founder proposing that they should go and see the men digging the foundations out, he walked with them to the old place.

As they walked down to the garden, Gil's

mind ran a good deal upon the thought that had occurred to him, but he said nothing, and waited patiently for his opportunity.

The visit was prolonged till towards evening, when, before returning, the founder walked down the narrow lane by the side of the Pool towards the meadow where Sir Mark had made his first proposal to Mace.

The place was full of memories for Gil, and he sighed as he thought of the bright sweet face he had encountered, and recalled his jealous feelings towards the man who had forced himself into the position of his rival.

But his attention was taken up directly after by the founder, who, with a return of his old business briskness, thrust open the meadow gate, and pointed to the new, sweetly-scented stack of hay just formed.

"What think you of that, Master Peasegood?" he said.

"Truly I am no judge of grass or hay, friend Cobbe, unless it be metaphorically, and for simile's sake—grown up at noon, cut down at night "—was the reply. " Ask our gossip, Tom Croftly here."

" Ay, Tom Croftly is a good judge of grass and stock too, though he is only a founder."

" I see not why a man may not be a judge of hay as well as iron," said Master Peasegood, as Croftly drove a horse and rough tumbril through the gate, and along the track to where the old stack of hay stood, with a good quarter of it cut away, waiting the knife.

" Neither do I," said the founder, smiling as he thought of his own business.

" You hear this, friend Gil Carr," said Master Peasegood ; " why not give up thy roving ways, and settle down to help friend Cobbe. There, lad, the good time is coming : the past forgotten ; sweet little Mace will be herself again ; and Master Cobbe will be ready to take thee by the hand as son.

Faith, and how deftly Tom Croftly handles that great blade, and cuts the hay in squares. Were I a fighting man, methinks that would be a good weapon to have in battle. Heyday! what ails the man? Does he want to break his neck?"

For Tom Croftly suddenly threw up his hands, leaped some eight feet down into the meadow, and came up panting and with his forehead bedewed with sweat. His eyes were staring, and his countenance ghastly, while for a few moments he could not speak.

"Hast seen a ghost, Tom Croftly?" cried Master Peasegood with a hearty laugh.

"Close upon it, master," gasped Croftly. "Hey, master, but it be terrifying."

"What is terrifying?" cried the founder.

"That, that," panted the man. "Lord forgive me; I didn't know what I did."

"Speak out, man, speak out," cried the founder, as the poor fellow began to tremble;

and he clutched him by the arm, fearing that some new trouble had befallen his house.

"I can't, yet, master, it be too terrify-ing," gasped Croftly. "The Lord forgive me for doing such a deed!"

"Less of that last, Tom Croftly, and more explanation," said Master Peasegood, sternly.

"Yes, Mas' Peasegood, I'll tell thee," gasped the poor fellow. "I sharpened up as usual—the big knife, you know—and went to cut the 'lowance for the horse and pony, when I couldn't have been looking; and he must have got up there to sleep."

"He? Who? What?" cried the founder.

"It's not I as can say, master," stam-mered the poor fellow; "the knife went down hard, but I thrust the more, and then, taking up the truss of hay, his head rolled down."

"What?" roared the founder.

"Heaven forgive me, master," cried Croftly, sinking on his knees, "I've cut a man's head clean from his body."

The founder and Master Peasegood stared at him aghast, as if believing he was mad, but the poor fellow was sane enough; and, on following him to the little stack, there was the horrible truth; but Croftly was relieved on finding his knife had decapitated the dead, and not some sleeping man.

"Was he dead, then?" he faltered, in answer to a few words spoken by Master Peasegood.

"Dead, man! ay, months ago. Heaven have mercy on us, it's a horrible thing."

"You're right," said the founder, turning away with a shudder; "the poor wretch must have lain down when we were making the stack, and more hay have been thrown upon him. He must have been smothered."

"Some gipsy, perhaps," said Master Peasegood, whose broad face looked white.

"Here be a bottle by him," said Tom

Croftly, lifting one from beside the body, "and here be a strap. Why, master, master!" he cried, rising up with a scrap of clothing in his hand.

"What is it, Tom?" said the founder, shuddering. "Come away, man, come away."

"Ay, I'll come away, Mas' Cobbe, but I've found out who it be."

"You have?" cried Master Peasegood, excitedly, as the man opened and smelt the bottle.

"Ay, I have, said Croftly. "That be strong waters in this bottle; and him as lay down," he continued, sagaciously, "I say, him as lay down upon that half-built stack was drunk, and the steam of the moist hay stifled him."

"But who think you it was?" cried the founder.

"Him as was missed," cried Croftly, triumphantly.

"Thank God!" cried Master Peasegood; "then Gil was as innocent as the day."

"Innocent—as the day?" cried the founder, in a puzzled voice, as he looked from one to the other. "Poor creature, how do you know? But I don't understand. Some one who was missed? Good God!" he cried, as a light flashed upon him, and he took a step or two up the short ladder by the stack, and then leaped down. "'Tis Abel Churr!"

CHAPTER XIX.

HOW GIL CARR LIT THE LAMPS OF LOVE.

ANOTHER year slipped by and Gil's ship had made a couple more voyages with Wat Kilby at the helm, for Culverin Carr had stayed at home, the helper and adviser of Jeremiah Cobbe. The Pool-house had risen again from its ashes, stone for stone, beam for beam, in spite of the bitter curse fulminated against those who should restore it. The aspect of age could not be given to the place, but it was a labour of love on the founder's part to consult with Gil how they should get that clump of roses, that high cluster of clematis, and those bright flowers to grow beneath the window as of old.

Wealthy as he was, the founder could replace many things destroyed by the calamity that befel his house, and with so zealous a treatment it was wonderful how nearly they brought the new house in furniture and surroundings to resemble the old.

At last they paused, feeling that there was nothing more to do, and the two strong men sat at the table in the big parlour, gazing the one into the other's face, as if to ask for hope and friendly assurance of success. For on the next day Mace was to be brought to the new house, and they both felt that, if her mind were to be restored, they must see some symptoms in the change.

The founder begged Gil to help him bring his child home once more, but he bluntly refused.

"Nay," he said; "I will not come. Take her thyself. Thou art her father, and God speed thee in the task."

It was a glorious summer day at the end of July, when the flowers were blooming, and the whole air was redolent with Nature's sweetest scents. The Pool was pure as crystal, and amidst the broad green leaves the silver chalices of the water-lilies swam upon the surface, where the herons waded, and the gorgeous kingfisher darted across the glassy mirror.

In the old garden the flowers drooped their heads in the heat which quivered over the grassy meads, while the forest-trees were silent in the glowing sunshine. No leaf moved, no zephyr played in the dark shades, but lizard and glistening beetle darted here and there, where the sandstone peered out amidst the heaths and ferns.

Mace suffered herself to be led by her father from the cottage they had made their home; but she heeded not the faces at the window and door, nor heard the pitying words spoken concerning her by the work-people who had eaten her father's bread for years.

They watched her as the grey-headed founder led her across the bridge, and opened the garden gate; but she did not look. He spoke to her and pointed out her favourite trees, and then groaned in the anguish of his heart, for she made no reply. Her soft, sweet eyes might have been blind ; her tongue have never spoken ; and her soft, pinky, shell-like ears have never heard a sound, for all the sign she gave ; and the founder's heart sank low as he felt that his task of love had been labour in vain.

And yet he would not despair; but, leading her in, he gently placed her in the recess by the open window with her work spread around as of old, and her roses nodding and flinging their odours into the pleasant room.

No word, no look, no sign ; and at last, in despair, the founder left her with her maid, and, bent of head and weary, trudged up to Master Peasegood's cot to tell of his disappointment over a friendly pipe.

" Yes," he said, at last; " it is all over, and I am going to try to be resigned."

" Nay," said the parson, " why say that? Be resigned, man, come to you what may ; but, after all this preparation, why give it up ? "

" Because it is useless, Master Peasegood. Her mind is dead."

Master Peasegood refilled a pipe, and lit it to smoke for awhile in silence, while the founder gazed before him through the open window at the setting sun.

" I could preach thee a long, long sermon on the subject of hope, Master Cobbe," said the parson at last; "but I will refrain. Look here, man, and recollect what thou hast done. Only to-day thou did'st take our sweet smitten flower back to the bed where it blossomed and grew so fair. It had been away in desert soil that had blighted it, and where it had grown wild and strange; and, lo! thou saidst 'I will plant it back in the old sweet soil, and there shall be a miracle; it shall blossom in an instant as of old—in the twinkling of an eye.'"

"Yes, yes, I did—I did," cried the founder, sadly.

"And it did not blossom a bit," said Master Peasegood bluntly. "Jeremiah Cobbe, that is all."

"All!" cried the founder, blankly.

"Yes, all at present. Wait, man; wait, and be reasonable. Such a thing as thou askest of Heaven must be the result of time, or some stronger power than thine. We have miracles enough now-a-days, for every work of God is miraculous; but we have no sacred conjuring tricks in common life. Heaven forgive me if I am irreverent. I mean we have no such sudden changes as you expected here. Tut, man, wait awhile and have some faith. I'd have more faith in a tender kiss and a loving word from Gil, than in all that thou canst do. Wait, man, wait. Maybe he is already working at that which proved a sorry failure in thy fatherly hands."

" He refused to come," said the founder, sadly.

" Ay, with thee ; but maybe he has stolen to her side now thou art here."

" Dost think so ? "

" Nay, I know not; but fill thy pipe, man, and wait. I have faith that our darling was not restored to us for such a life in death as this. I' faith, friend Cobbe, I pray nightly that I may see some merry little prattlers with the faces of Gil and Mace, softened and sweet, playing round our chairs as we grow more wrinkled and more old. Heaven bless us! There's time enough yet. See here, man," he cried, rising and taking a curious flask and glasses from a corner cupboard, " here is some strange liquor sent me by Father Brisdone, a great man, now, in sunny France. He bids me wish him well when I drink thereof, and I do, and pray for his health and life. There," he continued as he filled the glasses, "here's Father Brisdone, and now here's Culverin Carr and his dear wife and children, bless them all."

"All," said the founder, fervently, as he drained his glass of the potent liquor; and then, as the evening crept on apace and the stars came blinking out, the two friends sat and smoked, with the founder's heart growing cheery from the words and liquor of his firm old friend.

It was as dark as a summer night knows how to be, when, after a final pipe, the founder rose to go.

"Nay, but I'll see thee home," said Master Peasegood; "and what is more, as it is early yet, I'll drink a flagon of ale and ask a blessing in the dear old—new—old—well, the to-be happy home ;" and rising he strolled down the lane with his friend and across the bridge.

The founder opened the gate and let his companion through with a strange sensation at his breast, and he was about to lead the way round to the door when Master Peasegood's hand was laid upon his shoulder, and with a hoarse sob he sank upon his knees, and buried his face in his hands, weeping like a child.

It was almost dark when Gil Carr, who had seen the founder go, strolled slowly down towards the Pool-house. He was heart-sick and weary, and the soft, balmy, night-air seemed filled with depressing influences. Another disappointment and another, and hope more distant still.

The night mists were rising, and he smiled sadly as he glanced at the dark and dewy banks, and thought of the long-ago, when, with a love of the hidden and secret, he and Mace had held stolen meetings, till she chided him and bade him come no more.

"Hah, but they were happy days," he sighed, as he walked on and on till he stood beside the wide-spreading Pool, and thought of his narrow escape from death therein. Then a few steps further, and he was by the rushing outlet where the water dashed under the little bridge and onward to the dripping wheel.

"Where are Sir Mark and his fair wife now?" he muttered, as with a faint smile he thought of the knight's plunge in the rushing stream, and his own to fish him out.

Again a few steps and he was across the bridge, leaning on the garden gate, and gazing sadly at the new casement that had replaced the old.

Yes, it was well done, and he thought of his many meetings, of his waiting that night

to carry his love away; then of the fight,
the explosion, and his scorching ordeal as he
clambered in and bore out her whom he
believed to be poor Mace.

Sad thoughts—sweet thoughts—thoughts
that almost unmanned him, so that when the
moon rose, and he gazed still at the casement,
he believed he was deceived, and that it was
not Mace there, but some trick of the imagination.

There was the figure at the open window,
and he was about to speak, but he checked
himself, and stole away.

Hastily recrossing the bridge, he hurried
along the lane, stooping gently here and
there, and returning in a few minutes to
bend over the tall bank facing the broad
casement of the Pool-house.

In a moment after, diamond-wise, there
shone forth from the dark grass four glowworms' lamps, the old love-signal of the past,
and with beating heart—he knew not why—

Gil retraced his steps, crossed the bridge, entered the garden, and, with his hands trembling, made his way towards where he could dimly make out the pale, sweet face in the halo of silver hair.

There was a rough, short ladder hard by, where Tom Croftly had helped to nail up the blossoming roses, close round Sweet Mace's panes; and Gil seized these rough garden steps as he stopped beneath, gazing with all his soul at the face of her he loved.

Was it a dream, or was it honest truth? Did he breathe and live and hear? Was he blind, or was she leaning out towards him, with outstretched hands, as her dear voice whispered with all the passion of her old, old love, the one word—

" Gil ? "

" Mace ! " he cried, and with a bound he sprang to her side, to clasp her to his breast, as her own soft, round arms drew his face closer—closer to hers, and their lips met in one long, loving kiss.

Miracle ?   Merely such a one as love might perform ; and when—how much later no one knew — the founder and Master Peasegood came slowly up, they saw and heard enough to make the latter's heart swell with joy as the father sank upon his knees in thankfulness for the blessing that had come at last.

THE END.

Nichols and Sons, Printers, 25, Parliament Street, Westminster.